1984

SHERWOOD ANDERSON

THE TELLER'S TALES

Selection and Introduction by
FRANK GADO

SIGNATURE SERIES

Union College Press
Schenectady, New York

Copyright to the Sherwood Anderson selections in this volume is held by Eleanor Copenhaver Anderson. These selections appear in THE TELLER'S TALES through special arrangement with Harold Ober Associates.

Standard Book Number: 0-912756-09-8

Library of Congress Catalog Card Number: 83-51481

"I Want to Know Why" (first published in *The Smart Set,* November 1919; first collected in THE TRIUMPH OF THE EGG, 1921).

"The Egg" (*The Dial,* March 1920; THE TRIUMPH OF THE EGG).

"The Other Woman" (*The Little Review,* July 1920; THE TRIUMPH OF THE EGG).

"Milk Bottles" (first published under the title "Why There Must Be a Midwestern Literature" in *Vanity Fair,* March 1921; HORSES AND MEN, 1923).

"The Form of Things Concealed" (published as the Foreword to HORSES AND MEN).

"The Man Who Became a Woman" (HORSES AND MEN).

"Death in the Woods" (*The American Mercury,* September 1926; DEATH IN THE WOODS, 1933).

"Another Wife" (*Scribner's Magazine,* December 1926; DEATH IN THE WOODS).

"In a Strange Town" (*Scribner's Magazine,* January 1930; DEATH IN THE WOODS).

"There She Is—She Is Taking Her Bath" (DEATH IN THE WOODS).

"Brother Death" (DEATH IN THE WOODS).

"The Corn Planting" (*The American Magazine,* November 1934; THE SHERWOOD ANDERSON READER 1947).

"Daughters" (THE SHERWOOD ANDERSON READER).

First printing of THE TELLER'S TALES: 1983

Contents

Introduction

What Whitman had been to an American poetry searching
for its own voice, Anderson was to the new American fiction in
the period after the First World War. Squads of young writers
carried copies of *Winesburg, Ohio* as though it were the recognition badge of a new fraternal order, and most responded in
some way to his influence while learning to resolve their particular visions. But if those engaged in "making it new" instinctively understood the revolutionary nature of his work, the
scholars, assessing it after the fact, have disagreed over its
significance and fundamentally distorted its motives.

Although Anderson occupies a prominent place in historical
commentaries on the "Revolt from the Village" that scrutinized
the small towns of the Mid-West, his differences from the
writers identified by that rather omnibus classification are far
more radical than the characteristics they share. When the
topic is Realism, he is tied to such writers as Willa Cather and
Ellen Glasgow, but Realism presumes the replication of reality
by art, and although he draws from life, his art is not mimetic.
His homage to Dreiser, coupled with his long line of characters
buffeted by forces they neither understand nor control, has
prompted some literary historians to insert him among the
Naturalists; the objectivity and deterministic philosophy that
are cardinal marks of Naturalism, however, are quite remote
from his concerns. Often called "the American D. H. Law-
rence," he was one of the first to deal openly with sex, but his
interests in the subject are not essentially Laurentian — nor,

despite the claims of observers seeking to demonstrate literature's response to the intellectual currents of the 'twenties, is his treatment of repressed desires Freudian, in any valid sense, in more than a few instances. Most commonly, those who regard the changed view of language itself as a prime sign of the century's new writing point to him as the bridge from Mark Twain to Faulkner and (with Gertrude Stein) to Hemingway; even so, his concept of words in the tracing of forms bespeaks an aesthetic engineering basically unlike theirs. All these attempts to fix him within a category exaggerate superficial or secondary attributes, and in so doing, miss the originality of his genius.

But the biographers and literary historians, even though they have skewed their reports, have at least tried to deal with Anderson; the critics, in contrast, have generally been chary of him. One reason may be that his works do not easily lend themselves to the methodologies successively fashionable in academe — from the New Criticism to the latest vogue from New Haven. A more persuasive explanation, however, resides in the fact that Anderson's talent lay principally in the short story.

If America did not invent the short story, it did transform the genre and dominate its modern development. Yet our critics have tended to slight its importance in American letters, perversely treating it as though it were a lower species of fiction. While studies of the art of the novel spread unrelentingly across library shelves, studies of the art of the short story remain few and quite inferior. Among those considered major writers, Poe alone has earned recognition primarily for his short fiction. Hawthorne's tales are often artistically and psychologically more complex than his novels — and more profoundly at the center of the American psyche — but it is Hawthorne the novelist who has drawn the greater attention. James preferred "the blest *nouvelle*," but critical discussions of his works usually only allude to his short stories in the course of examining the novels. All that is of value in Hemingway can be found in his stories, which are genuinely in the front rank of this century's literature; his reputation, however, still rests on his novels — formally uninteresting performances that seem more mannered and pretentious with every rereading. If, as in the case of a Peter Taylor or a Grace Paley, a gifted writer chooses to be constant to the short story, critical neglect is virtually certain. Inversely, a well-established success in the novel can insure that the writer's stories will enjoy a popularity exceeding their intrinsic merit (e.g., Fitzgerald's stories — which, apart from scattered passages of brilliant prose, reflect a sophomoric mind and a technically clumsy composer).

This bias has been especially damaging to the perception of Anderson. He wrote novels because they held out hope of financial security (a will o' the wisp he chased throughout most of his career as an artist), not because he felt an affinity towards the genre. (*Poor White*, a valuable document reflecting America's painful emergence from its agrarian chrysalis, is the best realized of these efforts, but even here, he struggles unsuccessfully with novelistic practice in the setting, narrative advance, and, most conspicuously, form.) Yet, when the critic looks beyond *Winesburg,* his eye invariably trains on the novels, the province of fiction where Anderson is at his weakest—indeed, the predisposition is so strong that even *Winesburg* is treated as though it were a kind of novel, with almost all critical concern riveted to its continuing characters and themes rather than to the construction of the individual pieces. The reverse side of this prejudice, of course, is a crimped view of the short fiction. In his recent book on the short story, Walter Allen concedes, grudgingly, that Anderson is central to the American tradition of story writing, but he never bothers to explain why; more curious still, he confines his comments to *Winesburg* — which, although it looms over the rest of Anderson's books, contains neither his most representative nor his best short stories. Unfortunately, Allen's constricted vision is not atypical.

When Allen calls him simplistic — "a *naif* and at times … a *faux naif*" — or Frederick J. Hoffman speaks of his words coming "together in an unconscious process of creative illiteracy," one hears the echo of attacks first mounted in the 'twenties and repeated with devastating effect by Lionel Trilling in 1941. Anderson, they claimed, lacked precision, aesthetic refinement, and intellectual depth; his fiction appealed to adolescent sensibilities and proferred easy solutions to complex

problems. To be sure, the novels often warrant such dispar-
agements, but his finest stories (and it is presumably the succes-
ses that reveal an artist's measure) most emphatically do not.
Far from dealing in solutions, they reach for a heightened
awareness of vital mysteries, and their constructions are intri-
cate and often elegant.

In his most-quoted remark, Anderson blasted the contrived
stories he called "the bastard children of de Maupassant, Poe,
and O. Henry." There were, he insisted, "no plot short stories
ever lived in any life"; consequently, there are no plots in
Anderson's stories, either. But this does not mean that they are
loose, aimless affairs. The short story has traditionally oper-
ated according to realistic assumptions: regardless of its type,
from the so-called fairy tale to the Naturalists' "experiments," it
implicitly claimed to reflect the world it postulated. That which
defined the story — made beginning, middle, and end one
piece — was the presentation of events in such a way that *the
events themselves* became invested with meaning; plot, the nexus
of elements described by movement in time, depended upon
the author's selection and manipulation, but the story remained essentially a report from the world. Anderson over-
turned the conventions to liberate the fiction from the deter-
minants of time and incident. In his scheme, the story resides
not in events or even solely in the relationship between the
teller and the thing narrated but in its being told. Although
sequentiality is an inescapable quality of narrative, in Anderson the sequence of particulars responds to an urgency quite
independent from the usual chronological impulse.

An equally important aspect of his departure from realism
has to do with his concept of language. A passage in "Loneli-
ness," one of the more autobiographical sections in *Winesburg*,
comments directly on the relationship between the artist and
the world he imitates. The story's central character (who, like
the author himself, paints scenes of Winesburg) hears his work
praised, but the admiration exasperates him because it has a
false premise: "You don't get the point ... the picture you see
doesn't consist of the things you see and say words about." As
with Anderson's stories, what it does "consist of" is a "hidden
knowledge"—"the beginning of everything" that brings images

into configuration but cannot itself be imaged. Concern with how the word evokes its referent was a preoccupation of expatriate literary circles, and Anderson's focus on what lies beneath the surface seems, initially, to anticipate Hemingway's "iceberg theory"—the idea that the eighth part that is visible in writing must be supported by the seven-eighths the writer knows and yet does not describe. Actually, however, the two take opposite positions. While Hemingway realized that an excess of words would blunt the reader's sensitivity, he nonetheless believed that presenting the essential would enable the reader to supply the missing details, and thus restore the writer's original perception in full. In Anderson, the hidden knowledge remains hidden (even from the author) because its ramifications and implications lie beyond language's power of containment; it excites the current of energy that flows from the story's source to its conclusion, but neither the source nor the conclusion—nor, even, the connecting material—can depict it. Whereas Hemingway condenses language to intensify what the early decades of the century fashionably called its *quiditas*, Anderson, stressing the irreducibility of the word to experience, allows it to expand, apparently uncontrolled, as though it were searching for its uncertain object.

Anderson's idiosyncratic conception of narrative emerges most clearly where he operates at the farthest remove from conventional structures. "In a Strange Town" is a prime example. Although the opening statement, "A morning in a country town in a strange place," seems nothing more than a simple stage direction establishing the setting, its actual purpose is to imply a question that will pulse through the rest of the story: Why does the narrator repeatedly leave his home to wander in unfamiliar surroundings? After several paragraphs in which he notes the chorus and dance of the living world, the narrator supplies a simple answer: being alone among strangers, he says, whets a sense of wonder that his rubbing against the familiar has dulled. But this assertion, the reader gradually realizes, masks as well as reveals, and the same compulsive garrulousness that betrays his reluctance to speak the whole truth also makes it difficult to surmise what that underlying urgency may be. (Indeed, Anderson's strategy of indirection misorients the reader into assuming this floatation of utterances is unmoored to authorial artifice.) Eventually, however, as if to slice through the confusion he has created, the narrator returns to the subject he had posed at the long monologue's start:

> A while ago I was speaking of a habit I have formed of going suddenly off like this to some strange place. "I have been doing it ever since it happened," I said. I used the expression "it happened."
>
> Well what happened?
>
> Not so very much.

"It," he then explains, was a car accident that killed a female student who used to visit the narrator, a philosophy professor, in his office. Although he insists "she was nothing special to me," the womanly girl had roused thoughts long stilled by his wife and the others who populate his days. Yet, on receiving the news of the accident, he showed no emotion — his only response was to ride a train into the countryside.

The solution to the puzzle introduced in the story's initial sentence has finally fallen into place. Contrary to what the reader may immediately infer when the "secret" is told, these ritual excursions do not express a form of mourning for the girl's death (which he deems "not so very much"), nor are they just the result of a naive wanderlust as he first suggests. Something else, related to both but different from either, is at work here: a need to recreate the stirring of vitality he felt in that brief moment when her life touched his. In this respect, the narrator's recitation of his curious adventures represents an act of affirmation; beginning with a celebration of life's fullness and concluding with the evocation of a friend's death, it is an elegy in which the usual order is reversed.

But if analyzing the story in this way reveals its formal outline, it does not constitute a paraphrase. Few of Anderson's stories lend themselves to such translation since their textual statements usually operate as refractions of the mind and the being submerged beneath the level of language. Typically, "In a Strange Town" makes this underlying reality manifest through the tensions among contrarieties, none of which is wholly true or false. The narrator describes his trips as baths in life, yet, relishing being alone among strangers, he scarcely immerses himself in their lives. He claims to like people's thinking him odd because it will stimulate "a little current" of curiosity; yet his suppression of his own curiosity about the inhabitants of the mysterious house on his street also shows that he is intimidated by the label. He preaches against the false faces human beings show to each other; yet, as a stranger intruding into the rhythm of life in the town, he associates himself with someone who passed bad checks among its citizens. Paradoxically, he knows "too much and not enough" about those he observes; although he seeks communion with them by expanding his knowledge of their inner experience, he also admits that what he knows blunts his interest in them. The most significant of the many contradictions, however, involves the presumptive accumulated meaning of the story itself. The narrator proclaims his love of life while he repeatedly sneers at the importance accorded death by those who lead unquickened lives. Yet a careful reading discloses his own preoccupation with death and his haunting awareness that he is "no longer young"; moreover, far from exhibiting a celebrant in the mass of humanity, his almost furtive demeanor in the strange towns attests a crabbed and frightened psyche. Anderson's purpose is not to establish his narrator's "unreliability"; rather, it is to array statement against itself, to reveal the narrator—our deputy—as life's fool.

If any one coupling of theme and structure in Anderson's short fiction is paradigmatic, it is this progress to a culminative moment in which the reader empathically perceives a character's utter vulnerability and confusion. Anderson employs various strategies toward this end, but behind each lies the universal nightmare of the self discovering its nakedness before the world.

As "I Want to Know Why" shows, this nightmarish quality often arises from a sexual context. The story seems another instance of the initiation motif that is so characteristic of the period's fiction; indeed, one recognizes a number of conventions in its movement from the narrator's expressions of his unwitting wish to remain a child, to a climactic event that simultaneously confirms his innocent intuition and prefigures

its inevitable loss, to his bewilderment on discovering his sur-
rogate father's "rottenness." Even so, Anderson departs from
the usual pattern: the narrator does not actually become an
initiate (none of Anderson's narrators is ever truly initiated
into the secrets of the tribe), nor is this adolescent's attainment
of sexual sophistication quite the point. Almost by definition,
the initiation story proceeds from ignorance to knowledge;
here, in contrast, the narrator begins with an account of his
sure moral judgment and ends with a confession of his uncertainty. A critical approach to "I Want to Know Why" virtually
requires consideration of the reasons for this inversion.

The implications of the conclusion appear self-evident: in
kissing the prostitute, Jerry Tillford has shown himself to be
just another adult, thereby betraying the narrator's trust in his
mentor's moral superiority; furthermore, since Jerry also
functions as an older alter-ego, his fall from grace anticipates
the narrator's encounter with his own "rottenness" as he ad-
vances into manhood. (Thus, it is not only Jerry but also life
that betrays the adolescent's innocent faith.) Nothing in the
ending violates the reader's expectations; in fact, Anderson has
specifically foreshadowed it by having the narrator, early in the
story, complain about a trick played on him. An adult had said
that eating half a cigar would stunt his growth, but the foul-
tasting remedy "did no good. I kept right on growing. It was a
joke." The same elements — anger at the treachery of adults,
despair over the inability to halt biological change, and fear of
not fitting into a mysterious scheme of life — recur in the
ending; in effect, it is the joke's complement.

But to see *merely* how this specific joke operates within the
story is not enough. The more significant observation, bearing
directly on Anderson's unorthodox practice, is that the
dynamics of the story itself are joke-like. Humor in general
deals figuratively with anxiety, and jokes in particular manifest
this anxiety not only in their subject matter but also in their
structure. The joke trades in subversion, especially in the
punch line's upsetting of assumptions; its action proceeds
along a double course that simultaneously confirms and violates its own logic. Although the result is scarcely funny, in "I
Want to Know Why," the story develops toward a similar state

of contradiction. The narrator urgently wants to "know why," yet, just as urgently, he tries to retreat from that knowledge. The reader immediately knows the "why's" that cause the narrator's distress, yet, from a farther remove, the more profound questions raised about human behavior remain unanswered— and unanswerable. On the one hand, the conclusion implies the reassurance that the narrator's confusion will disappear when, inevitably, he attains the reader's level of sophistication; on the other, it induces a longing for return to innocence.

Although critics commonly speak of Anderson's "ambiguity," the term is seldom appropriate. His characters are often frustrated in their efforts to unriddle their circumstances, but the stories themselves neither turn on the possibility of alternative interpretations nor show their author to be equivocal or unsteady in his purpose. What is mislabeled ambiguity might better be described as a method of "*anti*guity." In "There She Is—She Is Taking Her Bath," for example, John Smith, the troubled husband who narrates the story, has hired a detective to collect evidence of his wife's infidelity; then, afraid of being forced to act when the proof will be delivered, he has returned to the agency pretending to be his wife's lover and bribed the detective's partner to falsify the report. The initial motive underlying the story's action drives toward certainty; the second reverses direction to re-establish uncertainty. But the sum of the actions is zero only in respect to the husband's question about his wife's chastity, and contrary to first impressions and at least one critic's inference,* the story is not about whether Mrs. Smith is unfaithful but about her husband's insistence that life conform to codes of behavior. Smith admires "men who, like myself, ... keep the world going"; as a paragon of those "of some account in the world," he cites an expert on the rules of whist. Rules are very important to Smith; in fact, it is not jealousy that stirs him but the thought that his wife believes she can *cheat* with impunity — and, still

---

*In the introduction to his collection of Anderson's short stories, Maxwell Geismar reads the conclusion as saying: "Who wants to know about such things?"—i.e., that this is a tale designed with a caution against curiosity as its moral.

worse, with a "young squirt" who flouts the work ethic and thus makes fools of those who shoulder their responsibilities. That she should be casually taking a bath (instead of trembling with a guilty conscience) when he is about to confront her with his justified suspicions shakes his faith in an invisible order that governs all existence. Furthermore, Smith's tenuous hold on self-esteem depends upon his membership in what he conceives to be the great confraternity of men, a lodge of "insiders" possessing the secret knowledge of how things are done. The closed bathroom door behind which his wife insouciantly bathes while his world is tottering defines him as an outsider, feckless before the greater mystery of woman.

Woman's power to expose the male as a fool often recurs as a theme in Anderson's fiction. Contemplating remarriage, the doctor in "Another Wife" vacillates between fear and desire. The woman is ten year his junior, yet, he imagines, she is far more experienced sexually; consequently, he sees himself in her eyes as at once an unattractive old man and a fumbling boy. He clings to the memory of his undemanding first wife as though it were an amulet; however, he also recalls somewhat ruefully that she had never excited him. To earn the new woman's respect, he feels he must rekindle his ambition, strive for professional success; at the same time, he yearns for rest from life's race. He wants to kiss her, but he is also afraid she wants to be kissed in order to trap him. This mental dance finally ends when, on returning to his cabin (presumably after proposing to her), he says, "Oh Lord — I've got me a wife, another wife, a new one." But if, in Aristotelian terms, this completes the action, it does not resolve the confusion within the doctor's psyche—which is the story's true subject. The last two sentences, significantly, consist of an exclamation of mixed emotion and a question: "How glad and foolish and frightened he still felt! Would he get over it after a time?" The same two sentences could serve as the conclusion to "The Other Woman," which focusses on the mind of a narrator who is torn between his attraction to a lower-class woman (with whom he feels sexually free) and his love for his bride (a "respectable woman" who asks him to delay consummation of their marriage until she has overcome her inhibitions). Clearly, the narrator's unsorted feelings toward these two women are similar to the doctor's abashment in "Another Wife" (particularly in respect to his two wives); in addition, the story's final image parallels that of "There She Is — She Is Taking Her Bath": although here it is an uncrossed *open* door that separates the narrator from his wife, the effect is almost the same.

Still another story that may be included in this group (despite differences in the manner in which it addresses its content) is "Daughters." Anderson repeatedly juxtaposes John Shepard's annoyance with his daughter Wave—whom he sees as wayward, headstrong, inconsiderate, and unfeminine—and his loving concern for her dutiful, mild, self-sacrificing sister Kate. Continuing throughout the recitation of Shepard's decline in fortunes, these comparisons seem tediously predictable and all-too-obviously foreshadow a violent outburst, directed at once against Wave and the injustice of life. Just such an explosion does occur at the close: after eavesdropping on the sharing of physical intimacies between Wave and a male boarder the family has taken in, the father almost chokes her to death. But the expected conclusion then develops an entirely unexpected signification. Shepard, the reader suddenly realizes, has subconsciously identified himself with the boarder, whom he had hoped might marry Kate—just the kind of woman he says he would have chosen for a wife. When the father sees this alter-ego fondling Wave, the implications are devastating: beneath the puritanical rage, and beneath the exacting of vengeance for what he construes to be a slight suffered by the "good" daughter, lies the far more powerful emotional storm roiled by the lust within him that Wave has aroused and he has repressed for years. Deepening the psychological dimension of this scene, Anderson describes it as though it were a dream that has become real. (If one stops short of pronouncing this lust incestual, it must at least be recognized as an unacknowledged desire for such unbridled, passionate women as Wave represents.) Then, finally, the author gives the screw yet another turn. While the father tries to fall asleep, he hears both daughters whispering and laughing behind the closed door of their room — perhaps about him. "There was something incomprehensible": their easy comradeship suggests that he has misread them, that Kate is really no different from Wave, that all women are alike in their harboring a luminous secret, and that its light exposes him as a fool.

Despite variations, the stories from "I Want to Know Why" to "Daughters" travel similar orbits and arrive at similar destinations. The most striking correspondence is in their concern with the sexual relationship between men and women and their use of that relationship as a mirror revealing the problematic nature of the self. What aggregates them as a constellation, however, is not subject or theme but a conception of structure that moves toward nullification rather than completion. Not all of Anderson's stories, of course, operate on the same principle (if they did, he would have been violating one of his favorite counsels for young writers: to avoid formulas of any sort.) Even so, his insistence on avoiding the "mechanical" in the composition of fiction fostered the development of anti-mechanical formulations that, although of different kinds, almost become conventions of their own. Thus, alongside a class of stories that rely on an "antiguous" structure, we find a group in which the antiguity inheres in a central symbol.

Perhaps the simplest example of this sort (if one can speak of simplicity in such an artfully complex performance) is "Milk Bottles." Superficially, the half-empty bottles of the milk that has been transported from the country to the city, where, in unrefrigerated apartments, it spoils in the summer heat, represent the lives of the people. Spiritually isolated from each other, these immigrants from the farms are "souring" in their struggle for success in Chicago. The reader soon perceives, however, that the symbolism is multistable. In each of the seven instances in which the bottles are mentioned, the signification changes. An even more pronounced shift occurs in the values revolving about the "milk" itself. Inspired by the bottles-of-sour-milk theme, the narrator's friend, an ad man, has written an account of a couple he took to be lovers until he heard them quarreling over money. When the narrator reads the crumpled pages of the story his friend has thrown away, he recognizes its worth as genuine literature, but to the ad man, it is trash that has served its purpose in priming the pump for his writing the "real stuff"—an over-blown piece of boosterism about "a cool-headed, brave people, marching forward to some spiritual triumph, the promise of which was inherent in the physical aspects of the town." The paradox is self-evident: the truth about the city dwellers, which is foul, is beautiful; the lie, which is beautiful, is foul. And wrapped around this paradox is another: the narrator appreciates the beauty in his friend's life, even though its conduct is based on delusion. The story manifestly celebrates the human, but in doing so, it undermines its own logic.

"The Egg," one of Anderson's three greatest works and a classic of American literature, also utilizes a multistable symbol which, as in "Milk Bottles," is indicated by the title. Clearly, the egg symbolizes life, but this identification scarcely settles the issue of its meaning, for life itself eludes meaning—which in turn *is* the story's "meaning." A symbol, by definition, implies relationship to a referent, yet in this context, the quest for the significance of the referents leads only back to the symbol. Initially, the egg suggests the folly of ambition and the absurdity of life. Next, it is associated with the narrator's father, marked as unmistakably ovoid by his bald head; the victim of his previous attempt to realize his ambitions (he is, in Anderson's idiosyncratic use of the word, a "grotesque"), the father now seeks to make up for his failure by opening a restaurant, where, on a shelf behind the counter, he exhibits bottles containing the grotesque accidents of nature that sometimes hatch from eggs. The saddest *lusus naturae* behind the counter, however, is really himself. Here, the egg develops still another implication. Misunderstanding the point of the anecdote about Columbus and the egg, the failing restaurant owner brands the discoverer of the New World a cheat and announces that he will make an egg stand on end without trickery. If there is justice, he thinks, the feat will win him the approbation of the world—synecdochically represented by one lonely customer. The weight of the entire story bears on this desperate scene as the father struggles to justify his life (and to redeem his faith in justice). Of course, the egg breaks, and in his wrathful acknowledgment of the utter frustration of his ambitions, the father hurls another egg at the customer, who is fleeing this drama of absurdity. The progression has come full circle.

But the joke is not yet played out. Shortly after beginning his account, the narrator had cautioned himself to tell the tale correctly, so that "it will center on the egg," not the hen. At the end, he reminds the reader that "from the egg came the hen who again laid the egg," and then states, "I am the son of my father." The significance in this combination of otherwise empty truisms is patent. Given that the course of the narrative corresponds to the cycle of egg and hen and egg, the egg now represents the son, and the story, "correctly told," finds the narrator at its center. "In the long nights when there was little to do, Father had time to think," he had commented midway through his tale. "That was his undoing." In the closing lines, it is the *son* who is thinking—and who is undone. When he was a child, he recalls, he had stared at an egg that lay on the table the night of the fiasco in the restaurant (and, perhaps, wondered why it could not be made to stand upright); in the final sentences, as an adult, he concedes that the problem of the egg, which "remains unsolved," has scored its "final triumph."

The crucial role of the narrator in "The Egg" illustrates a general principle that Anderson often preached to others and almost always followed in his own short fiction: form, he maintained, is a function of the *teller's* reaction to his materials. (His novels, it is worth noting, do not take their shape from this relationship—and thereby suffer egregiously from a failure of discipline.) More than any other trait or aesthetic practice, the tensions generated among the teller, the telling, and the content of the tale told are responsible for those qualities that are the hallmark of the Anderson short story. As one might therefore expect, most of his stories are written in first person, and even among the rest, many (e.g., "Another Wife" and "Daughters") employ a restrictive point of view that is virtually first person. The "I" is more important in some narratives than in others, however. Of the first person stories discussed above, all but two ("In a Strange Town" and "The Egg") *could* be rewritten in restrictive third person; although it would surely diminish their effectiveness, their essence would remain. But in the exceptions, the story actually consists in the act of telling.

(Unlike the possibility of an "I Want to Know Why" ending with "He was puzzled," or of a "There She Is—She Is Taking Her Bath" that describes the husband in the park after walking away from the bathroom door, a recasting of "The Egg" concluding with a third person statement that the egg had finally triumphed in the protagonist's family is an impossibility.) Furthermore, it is in the telling of these quintessentially first person stories—which, in addition, also include "The Man Who Became a Woman" and "Death in the Woods"—that the peculiar Andersonian condition of antiguity is vested; the telling creates a form by "unresolving" what the content (i.e., the narrator's construction of an objective reality) seems to have resolved.

As the narrator explicitly states in the text, relating the central episode of "The Man Who Became a Woman" is his substitute for going to confession. Although he is now a married adult, Herman Dudley continues to be haunted by the memory of that tremulous moment in adolescence when the issue of a safe passage into manhood was very much in doubt. The theme of ambivalent sexuality indicated by the title first surfaces in the account of his feelings about his gelding, Pick-it-boy: "I wished he was a girl sometimes or that I was a girl and he was a man." In itself, the intimacy was reassuring, but the presence of a younger horse (a stallion named O My Man) signals the advent of a new stage in life when the very comfort provided by that relationship could prove dangerous. (The names of the horses are suggestive, as are the syllables of the narrator's own name: *her, man,* and *dud.*)

The story's next phase — set outside the fairgrounds in a grimy mining town, a "hellhole" that gives him "the fantods and the shivers" for reasons he cannot articulate but which the reader knows have to do with the subterranean recesses of his mind—illustrates the danger. Although he associates himself with men by entering in the town's saloon, it is a lonesome, frightened girl's face that stares back at him when he peers into the bar's cracked mirror. His reaction, not shame but fright that others may notice, is most revealing—and foreshadows the next event. The crowd's taunting of the "cracked" man and his "queer-looking kid" validate Herman's fears of what might happen if his own "crack" were noticed, and although he sympathizes with the victims, he resents being entrusted with the boy as though he were a member of this family. But the truly shattering moment comes when the cracked man stomps on his tormentors. The violence terrifies him, in part, it seems, because it manifests the possibility of a previously-un-discovered capacity within himself; slinking out "like a thief or a coward, which perhaps I am," Herman retreats to Pick-it-boy's stable and "the best and sweetest feelings I've ever had in my whole life."

This regression, a sexual fantasy in which boy and horse enjoy a nuptial relationship, proves to be another foreshadow-ing of the consequences of indulging the imagination when the two Negro swipes interrupt his dreams and proceed to treat him like a girl. Although he is "scared," his reactions are those of a virgin female, frightened and yet also submissive—as his thinking of himself as "a kind of princess" attests. Just when a fateful "deflowering" is about to decide the nature of his iden-tity, however, he gives "a kind of wriggle" and, "as good luck would have it," slides through a hay hole. He has been reborn a man. Running "like a crazy man," he eventually stumbles into the skeleton of a horse that is lying in a boneyard on the skirts of the fairground. "A feeling like the finger of God running down your back and burning you clean" overcomes him. "It burned all that silly nonsense about being a girl right out of me. I screamed at last and the spell that was on me was broken." The next day, he makes his escape from the stables that repre-sent his youth, "out of the race horse and the tramp life for the rest of my days."

The psychosexual implications of Herman's nightmarish experience are too obvious to ignore, of course, and the fact that its narration has a clearly demarcated beginning, middle, and end increases the temptation to regard the story solely in those terms. To yield to it, however, would be to miss half the story—and the more important half at that. One must bear in mind that the Herman Dudley who is *compelled* to tell his tale is an adult. If his perilous adventure had truly reached a safe conclusion, as the final line states, why does the urge to confess the tale still cause him to wake screaming? Why does he re-

peatedly mention his marriage to Jessie as proof that everything has turned out "all right"? And perhaps most significant
of all, if only a full confession will exorcise his possession by the
memory, why does he refuse to confront the truth (e.g., in his
attempt to hide from the homosexual nature of the swipes'
attack by advancing the most improbable claim that they either
mistook him for a girl or were "maybe partly funning")? As
Irving Howe points out: "Herman Dudley may even be, as he
insists, a normal man, but to grant this somewhat desperate
claim is to record the precariousness and internal ambiguity of
adult normality itself. And this... is the particular achievement
of the story, that through a recollection of adolescence it subtly
portrays a complex state of adult emotion." Indeed, it may be
even more complex than Howe realizes. If the bones into
which Herman falls represent (in Howe's words) "the death of
his adolescent [and homosexual] love," they also represent
death itself; in this respect, the reader should note that the
burning "finger of God" is a "new terror," making him seem "to
myself dead." The told tale of one fearful passage *in* life suggests an untold tale of fear about the passage *from* life. This
is not to say, of course, that "The Man Who Became a Woman"
rests on a submerged allegory; rather, that the telling of the
story, by undermining the resolution it asserts, displaces a
specific fear with a general anxiety, and that herein lies the true
seat of the terror generated by the tale.

The counterpoint of narrative act and object becomes more
overt in "Death in the Woods," which, along with "The Egg"
and "The Man Who Became a Woman," is usually recognized
as the short story writer's outstanding work. That it was also
Anderson's own favorite and that he labored over it longer
than over any other story suggests as well that it best
exemplifies his theory and practice of short fiction. Quite
properly, anthologists have selected it to represent Anderson
more often than any other tale. With all this attention, one
would think that it has been clearly and widely understood;
however, the contrary seems the case. The notes in one recent
anthology, unfortunately all-too typically, state that it "packs
the history of a nameless old woman into a series of incidents.
By adopting the point of view of an impressionable young boy,

Anderson endows his narrative with suspense and innocence. ...The death of the old woman becomes a symbol of both waste and mercy." Aside from the questionable interpretation of the theme, the fact that the narrator is not a boy but a man, and the curious lapse in remembering that her name is Grimes, this description (quaintly subtending the heading "For Thought") commits the frequent misreading of the story as a synchronic presentation (albeit in piecemeal fashion) of Mrs. Grimes's life and death. Even so perceptive a critic as Howe entirely misses the mark when he states that "'Death in the Woods' has only one significant flaw: a clumsiness in perspective which forces the narrator to offer a weak explanation of how he could have known the precise circumstances of the old woman's death."

That the narrator does not know (and cannot have known) these precise circumstances is, precisely, the point—or, at least, the key to the point—of the story. The narrator was eyewitness only to the scene of her death, *after* her body had been removed and the dogs had returned to town. Although the story begins as though the narrator were reporting a series of facts about the woman, the presumption of certainty is steadily erased as the narrative proceeds, section by section. All the details are based either on hearsay or on inferences drawn from the lives of others; even his description of the discovery of the body is confected from what he has heard a hunter say— colored, further, by his listening to a report of that account by his brother (who, "it is likely," did not get the point).

Since Anderson's method is to have the tale ride on its own melting, it is the closing sentences of the last section, where the facticity of Mrs. Grimes's story has evanesced, that reveal its meaning:

> The whole thing, the story of the old woman's death, was to me as I grew older like music heard from far off. The notes had to be picked up slowly one at a time. Something had to be understood. ...
> ... A thing so complete has its own beauty.
> I shall not try to emphasize the point. I am only explaining why I was dissatisfied then and have been ever since. I speak of that only that you may understand why I have been impelled to try to tell the simple story over again.

The image of the woman—old and exhausted yet strangely young as she lies dead in the snow, circled by the running dogs that deputize for all the living creatures who have depended on her providing for them—has captured the narrator's imagination because of the beauty in its completeness. Mrs. Grimes has only precipitated that image, which, in its composition of contrarieties, represents the mystery of life. In the final sense, however, what the story is "about" is not the emblem but the need to retell the story, over and over again; not a meaning itself but the search for a means to understand it. The true story never ends; it is a figure that enlarges as it fills with the experience of one's life.

If the preceding short stories illustrate the body of Anderson's original genius in the genre, the last two stories in this collection, "Brother Death" and "The Corn Planting," stand as a coda. Not only in their structure and use of symbolism but even in their narrative conception, they adhere to the conventional; the etching of a statement supersedes the unfolding of an antiguity. Both of these stories are homiletic at their core, and although they are emotionally powerful and skillfully executed, they spring more from the preacher than from the artist.

"Brother Death" brings to mind the stories of another preacher, the Tolstoy of *Twenty-three Tales*. Essentially, it is a parable. John Grey cuts down the shade trees to break his son Don's resistance to his will: "Something in you must die before you can possess and command." When that "something" does die, Don is reborn as the father. The other son, Ted, is spared this rite because it is assumed that his weak heart will cause him to die before he reaches manhood. And indeed, a year or two after the beautiful oaks have been reduced to stumps, Ted does die. But: "having to die his kind of death, he never had to make the surrender his brother had made—to be sure of possessions, success, his time to command—would never have to face the more subtle and terrible death that had come to his older brother." In that final irony, the story's didactic meaning is fully resolved, and in the coincidence of the symbol of the two stumps with the action that ends in disclosure of the two brothers' contrasting fates, its design is closed.

"The Corn Planting," which retells Wordsworth's poem "Michael" in American terms, at first resembles "Milk Bottles" or "Death in the Woods" (with which it is often compared). But the narrator here functions simply as a reporter; his consciousness is in no way involved with the dynamics of the story as a figure of meaning. And, in a still more important difference, although all three stories focus on a symbol that alludes to the complex wonder of life, here, even though what the old couple "were up to in connection with the life in their field and the lost life in their son is something you can't very well make clear in words," the symbolism of that image is conclusive in regard to both the story's meaning and its form.

To say that neither "Brother Death" nor "The Corn Planting" evinces an idosyncratically Andersonian quality of storytelling is not, of course, to pronounce them *necessarily* inferior. On their own terms, they are engaging, well-wrought fictions, similar in several respects to the *Winesburg* stories he produced at the start of his literary career. (One cannot fail to notice the resemblance "Brother Death" bears to sections of the "Godliness" stories; and in its contraposing of urban dissoluteness to the telluric vitality of nature, "The Corn Planting" restates a theme that is interwoven throughout the *Winesburg* volume.) Nevertheless, the absence here of that special energy Anderson generates in his best work serves to accentuate his genius where it does achieve originality.

Frank Gado
Schenectady, New York

The Teller's Tales

The Form of Things Concealed

Did you ever have a notion of this kind — there is an orange, or say an apple, lying on a table before you. You put out your hand to take it. Perhaps you eat it, make it a part of your physical life. Have you touched? Have you eaten? That's what I wonder about.

The whole subject is only important to me because I want the apple. What subtle flavors are concealed in it — how does it taste, smell, feel? Heavens, man, the way the apple feels in the hand is something — isn't it?

For a long time I thought only of eating the apple. Then later its fragrance became something of importance too. The fragrance stole out through my room, through a window and into the streets. It made itself a part of all the smells of the streets. The devil! — in Chicago or Pittsburgh, Youngstown or Cleveland it would have had a rough time.

That doesn't matter.

The point is that after the form of the apple began to take my eye I often found myself unable to touch at all. My hands went toward the object of my desire and then came back.

There I sat, in the room with the apple before me, and hours passed. I had pushed myself off into a world where nothing has any existence. Had I done that, or had I merely stepped, for the moment, out of the world of darkness into the light?

It may be that my eyes are blind and that I cannot see.
It may be I am deaf.

My hands are nervous and tremble. How much do they tremble? Now, alas, I am absorbed in looking at my own hands.

With these nervous and uncertain hands may I really feel for the form of things concealed in the darkness?

In a Strange Town

A morning in a country town in a strange place. Everything is quiet. No, there are sounds. Sounds assert themselves. A boy whistles. I can hear the sound here, where I stand, at a railroad station. I have come away from home. I am in a strange place. There is no such thing as silence. Once I was in the country. I was at the house of a friend. "You see, there is not a sound here. It is absolutely silent." My friend said that because he was used to the little sounds of the place, the humming of insects, the sound of falling water — far-off — the faint clattering sound of a man with a machine in the distance, cutting hay. He was accustomed to the sounds and did not hear them. Here, where I am now, I hear a beating sound. Some one has hung a carpet on a clothesline and is beating it. Another boy shouts, far off — "A-ho, a-ho."

It is good to go and come. You arrive in a strange place. There is a street facing a railroad track. You get off a train with your bags. Two porters fight for possession of you and the bags as you have seen porters do with strangers in your own town.

As you stand at the station there are things to be seen. You see the open doors of the stores on the street that faces the station. People go in and out. An old man stops and looks. "Why, there is the morning train," his mind is saying to him.

The mind is always saying such things to people. "Look, be aware," it says. The fancy wants to float free of the body. We put a stop to that.

Most of us live our lives like toads, sitting perfectly still, under a plantain leaf. We are waiting for a fly to come our way. When it comes out darts the tongue. We nab it.

That is all. We eat it.

But how many questions to be asked that are never asked. Whence came the fly? Where was he going?

The fly might have been going to meet his sweetheart. He was stopped; a spider ate him.

The train on which I have been riding, a slow one, pauses for a time. All right, I'll go to the Empire House. As though I cared.

It is a small town—this one—to which I have come. In any event I'll be uncomfortable here. There will be the same kind of cheap brass beds as at the last place to which I went unexpectedly like this — with bugs in the bed perhaps. A traveling salesman will talk in a loud voice in the next room. He will be talking to a friend, another traveling salesman. "Trade is bad," one of them will say. "Yes, it's rotten."

There will be confidences about women picked up — some words heard, others missed. That is always annoying.

But why did I get off the train here at this particular town? I remember that I had been told there was a lake here — that there was fishing. I thought I would go fishing.

Perhaps I expected to swim. I remember now.

"Porter, where is the Empire House? Oh, the brick one. All right, go ahead. I'll be along pretty soon. You tell the clerk to save me a room, with a bath, if they have one."

I remember what I was thinking about. All my life, since that happened, I have gone off on adventures like this. A man likes to be alone sometimes.

Being alone doesn't mean being where there are no people. It means being where people are all strangers to you.

There is a woman crying there. She is getting old, that woman. Well, I am myself no longer young. See how tired her eyes are. There is a younger woman with her. In time that younger woman will look exactly like her mother.

She will have the same patient, resigned look. The skin will sag on her cheeks that are plump now. The mother has a large nose and so has the daughter.

There is a man with them. He is fat and has red veins in his face. For some reason I think he must be a butcher.

He has that kind of hands, that kind of eyes.

I am pretty sure he is the woman's brother. Her husband is dead. They are putting a coffin on the train.

They are people of no importance. People pass them casually. No one has come to the station to be with them in their hour of trouble. I wonder if they live here. Yes, of course they do. They live somewhere, in a rather mean little house, at the edge of town, or perhaps outside the town. You see the brother is not going away with the mother and daughter. He has just come down to see them off.

They are going, with the body, to another town where the husband, who is dead, formerly lived.

The butcher-like man has taken his sister's arm. That is a gesture of tenderness. Such people make such gestures only when someone in the family is dead.

The sun shines. The conductor of the train is walking

along the station platform and talking to the station-master. They have been laughing loudly, having their little joke.

That conductor is one of the jolly sort. His eyes twinkle, as the saying is. He has his little joke with every station-master, every telegraph operator, baggage man, express man, along the way. There are all kinds of conductors of passenger trains.

There, you see, they are passing the woman whose husband has died and is being taken away somewhere to be buried. They drop their jokes, their laughter. They become silent.

A little path of silence made by that woman in black and her daughter and the fat brother. The little path of silence has started with them at their house, has gone with them along streets to the railroad station, will be with them on the train and in the town to which they are going. They are people of no importance, but they have suddenly become important.

They are symbols of Death. Death is an important, a majestic thing, eh?

How easily you can comprehend a whole life, when you are in a place like this, in a strange place, among strange people. Everything is so much like other towns you have been in. Lives are made up of little series of cir-cumstances. They repeat themselves, over and over, in towns everywhere, in cities, in all countries.

They are of infinite variety. In Paris, when I was there last year, I went into the Louvre. There were men and women there, making copies of the works of the old masters that were hung on the walls. They were profes-sional copyists.

They worked painstakingly, were trained to do just that kind of work, very exactly.

And yet no one of them could make a copy. There were no copies made.

The little circumstances of no two lives anywhere in the world are just alike.

You see I have come over into a hotel room now, in this strange town. It is a country-town hotel. There are flies in here. A fly has just alighted on this paper on which I have been writing these impressions. I stopped writing and looked at the fly. There must be billions of flies in the world and yet, I dare say, no two of them are alike.

The circumstances of their lives are not just alike.

I think I must come away from my own place on trips, such as I am on now, for a specific reason.

At home I live in a certain house. There is my own household, the servants, the people of my household. I am a professor of philosophy in a college in my town, hold a certain definite position there, in the town life and in the college life.

Conversations in the evening, music, people coming into our house.

Myself going to a certain office, then to a class room where I lecture, seeing people there.

I know some things about these people. That is the trouble with me perhaps. I know something but not enough.

My mind, my fancy, becomes dulled looking at them.

I know too much and not enough.

It is like a house in the street in which I live. There is a particular house in that street—in my home town—I was formerly very curious about. For some reason the people who lived in it were recluses. They seldom came out of their house and hardly ever out of the yard, into the street.

Well, what of all that?

My curiosity was aroused. That is all.

I used to walk past the house with something strangely alive in me. I had figured out this much. An old man with a beard and a white-faced woman lived there. There was a tall hedge and once I looked through. I saw the man walking nervously up and down, on a bit of lawn, under a tree. He was clasping and unclasping his hands and muttering words. The doors and shutters of the mysterious house were all closed. As I looked, the old woman with the white face opened the door a little and looked out at the man. Then the door closed again. She said nothing to him. Did she look at him with love or with fear in her eyes? How do I know? I could not see.

Another time I heard a young woman's voice, although I never saw a young woman about the place. It was evening and the woman was singing — a rather sweet young woman's voice it was.

There you are. That is all. Life is more like that than people suppose. Little odd fragmentary ends of things. That is about all we get. I used to walk past that place all alive, curious. I enjoyed it. My heart thumped a little.

I heard sounds more distinctly, felt more.

I was curious enough to ask my friends along the street about the people.

"They're queer," people said.

Well, who is not queer?

The point is that my curiosity gradually died. I accepted the queerness of the life of that house. It became a part of the life of my street. I became dulled to it.

I have become dulled to the life of my own house, or my street, to the lives of my pupils.

"Where am I? Who am I? Whence came I?" Who asks himself these questions any more?

There is that woman I saw taking her dead husband away on the train. I saw her only for a moment before I walked over to this hotel and came up to this room (an entirely commonplace hotel room it is) but here I sit, thinking of her. I reconstruct her life, go on living the rest of her life with her.

Often I do things like this, come off alone to a strange place like this. "Where are you going?" my wife says to me. "I am going to take a bath," I say.

My wife thinks I am a bit queer too, but she has grown used to me. Thank God, she is a patient and a good-natured woman.

"I am going to bathe myself in the lives of people about whom I know nothing."

I will sit in this hotel until I am tired of it and then I will walk in strange streets, see strange houses, strange faces. People will see me.

Who is he?

He is a stranger.

That is nice. I like that. To be a stranger sometimes, going about in a strange place, having no business there, just walking, thinking, bathing myself.

To give others, the people here in this strange place, a little jump at the heart too — because I am something strange.

Once, when I was a young man I would have tried to pick up a girl. Being in a strange place, I would have tried to get my jump at the heart out of trying to be with her.

Now I do not do that. It is not because I am especially faithful—as the saying goes—to my wife, or that I am not interested in strange and attractive women.

It is because of something else. It may be that I am a bit dirty with life and have come here, to this strange place, to bathe myself in strange life and get clean and fresh again.

And so I walk in such a strange place. I dream. I let myself have fancies. Already I have been out into the street, into several streets of this town and have walked about. I have aroused in myself a little stream of fresh fancies, clustered about strange lives, and as I walked, being a stranger, going along slowly, carrying a cane, stopping to look into stores, stopping to look into the windows of houses and into gardens, I have, you see, aroused in others something of the same feeling that has been in me.

I have liked that. Tonight, in the houses of this town, there will be something to speak of.

"There was a strange man about. He acted queerly. I wonder who he was."

"What did he look like?"

At attempt to delve into me too, to describe me. Pictures being made in other minds. A little current of thoughts, fancies, started in others, in me too.

I sit here in this room in this strange town, in this hotel, feeling oddly refreshed. Already I have slept here. My sleep was sweet. Now it is morning and everything is still. I dare say that, some time today, I shall get on another train and go home.

But now I am remembering things.

Yesterday, in this town, I was in a barber shop. I got my

hair cut. I hate getting my hair cut.

"I am in a strange town, with nothing to do, so I'll get my hair cut," I said to myself as I went in.

A man cut my hair. "It rained a week ago," he said. "Yes," I said. That is all the conversation there was between us.

However, there was other talk in that barbershop, plenty of it.

A man had been here in this town and had passed some bad checks. One of them was for ten dollars and was made out in the name of one of the barbers in the shop.

The man who passed the checks was a stranger, like myself. There was talk of that.

A man came in who looked like President Coolidge and had his hair cut.

Then there was another man who came for a shave. He was an old man with sunken cheeks and for some reason looked like a sailor. I dare say he was just a farmer. This town is not by the sea.

There was talk enough in there, a whirl of talk.

I came out thinking.

Well, with me it is like this. A while ago I was speaking of a habit I have formed of going suddenly off like this to some strange place. "I have been doing it ever since it happened," I said. I used the expression "it happened."

Well, what happened?

Not so very much.

A girl got killed. She was struck by an automobile. She was a girl in one of my classes.

She was nothing special to me. She was just a girl—a woman, really—in one of my classes. When she was killed I was already married.

She used to come into my room, into my office. We

used to sit in there and talk.

We used to sit and talk about something I had said in my lecture.

"Did you mean this?"

"No, that is not exactly it. It is rather like this."

I suppose you know how we philosophers talk. We have almost a language of our own. Sometimes I think it is largely nonsense.

I would begin talking to that girl—that woman—and on and on I would go. She had gray eyes. There was a sweet serious look on her face.

Do you know, sometimes, when I talked to her like that (it is, I am pretty sure, all nonsense), well, I thought...

Her eyes seemed to me sometimes to grow a little larger as I talked to her. I had a notion she did not hear what I said.

I did not care much.

I talked so that I would have something to say.

Sometimes, when we were together that way, in my office in the college building, there would come odd times of silence.

No, it was not silence. There were sounds.

There was a man walking in a hallway, in the college building outside my door. Once when this happened I counted the man's footsteps. Twenty-six, twenty-seven, twenty-eight.

I was looking at the girl—the woman—and she was looking at me.

You see I was an older man. I was married.

I am not such an attractive man. I did, however, think she was very beautiful. There were plenty of young fellows about.

I remember now that when she had been with me like that — after she had left — I used to sit sometimes for hours alone in my office, as I have been sitting here, in this hotel room, in a strange town.

I sat thinking of nothing. Sounds came in to me. I remembered things of my boyhood.

I remembered things about my courtship and my marriage. I sat like that dumbly, a long time.

I was dumb, but I was at the same time more aware than I had ever been in my life.

It was at that time I got the reputation with my wife of being a little queer. I used to go home, after sitting dumbly like that, with that girl, that woman, and I was even more dumb and silent when I got home.

"Why don't you talk?" my wife said.

"I'm thinking," I said.

I wanted her to believe that I was thinking of my work, my studies. Perhaps I was.

Well, the girl, the woman, was killed. An automobile struck her when she was crossing a street. They said she was absent-minded — that she walked right in front of a car. I was in my office, sitting there, when a man, another professor, came in and told me. "She is quite dead, was quite dead when they picked her up," he said.

"Yes." I dare say he thought I was pretty cold and unsympathetic — a scholar, eh, having no heart.

"It was not the driver's fault. He was quite blameless."

"She walked right out in front of the car?"

"Yes."

I remember that at the moment I was fingering a pencil. I did not move. I must have been sitting like that for two or three hours.

I got out and walked. I was walking when I saw a train. So I got on.

Afterward I telephoned to my wife. I don't remember what I told her at that time.

It was all right with her. I made some excuse. She is a patient and a good-natured woman. We have four children. I dare say she is absorbed in the children.

I came to a strange town and I walked about there. I forced myself to observe the little details of life. That time I stayed three or four days and then I went home.

At intervals I have been doing the same thing ever since. It is because at home I grow dull to little things. Being in a strange place like this makes me more aware. I like it. It makes me more alive.

So you see, it is morning and I have been in a strange town, where I know no one and where no one knows me.

As it was yesterday morning, when I came here, to this hotel room, there are sounds. A boy whistles in the street. Another boy, far off, shouts "A-ho."

There are voices in the street, below my window, strange voices. Some one, somewhere in this town, is beating a carpet. I hear the sound of the arrival of a train. The sun is shining.

I may stay here in this town another day or I may go on to another town. No one knows where I am. I am taking this bath in life, as you see, and when I have had enough of it I shall go home feeling refreshed.

I Want to Know Why

We got up at four in the morning, that first day in the east. On the evening before we had climbed off a freight train at the edge of town, and with the true instinct of Kentucky boys had found our way across town and to the race track and the stables at once. Then we knew we were all right. Hanley Turner right away found a nigger we knew. It was Bildad Johnson who in the winter works at Ed Becker's livery barn in our home town, Beckersville. Bildad is a good cook as almost all our niggers are and of course he, like everyone in our part of Kentucky who is anyone at all, likes the horses. In the spring Bildad begins to scratch around. A nigger from our country can flatter and wheedle anyone into letting him do most anything he wants. Bildad wheedles the stable men and trainers from the horse farms in our country around Lexington. The trainers come into town in the evening to stand around and talk and maybe get into a poker game. Bildad gets in with them. He is always doing little favors and telling about things to eat, chicken browned in a pan, and how is the best way to cook sweet potatoes and corn bread. It makes your mouth water to hear him.

When the racing season comes on and the horses go to

the races and there is all the talk on the streets in the evenings about the new colts, and everyone says when they are going over to Lexington or to the spring meeting at Churchill Downs or to Latonia, and the horsemen that have been down to New Orleans or maybe at the winter meeting at Havana in Cuba come home to spend a week before they start out again, at such a time when everything talked about in Beckersville is just horses and nothing else and the outfits start out and horse racing is in every breath of air you breathe, Bildad shows up with a job as cook for some outfit. Often when I think about it, his always going all season to the races and working in the livery barn in the winter where horses are and where men like to come and talk about horses, I wish I was a nigger. It's a foolish thing to say, but that's the way I am about being around horses, just crazy. I can't help it.

Well, I must tell you about what we did and let you in on what I'm talking about. Four of us boys from Beckersville, all whites and sons of men who live in Beckersville regular, made up our minds we were going to the races, not just to Lexington or Louisville, I don't mean, but to the big eastern track we were always hearing our Beckersville men talk about, to Saratoga. We were all pretty young then. I was just turned fifteen and I was the oldest of the four. It was my scheme. I admit that and I talked the others into trying it. There was Hanley Turner and Henry Rieback and Tom Tumberton and myself. I had thirty-seven dollars I had earned during the winter working nights and Saturdays in Enoch Myer's grocery. Henry Rieback had eleven dollars and the others, Hanley and Tom had only a dollar or two each. We fixed it all up and laid low until the Kentucky spring meetings were over and some of our men, the sportiest ones, the ones we envied the most, had cut out — then we cut out too.

I won't tell you the trouble we had beating our way on freights and all. We went through Cleveland and Buffalo and other cities and saw Niagara Falls. We bought things there, souvenirs and spoons and cards and shells with pictures of the falls on them for our sisters and mothers, but thought we had better not send any of the things home. We didn't want to put the folks on our trail and maybe be nabbed.

We got into Saratoga as I said at night and went to the track. Bildad fed us up. He showed us a place to sleep in hay over a shed and promised to keep still. Niggers are all right about things like that. They won't squeal on you. Often a white man you might meet, when you had run away from home like that, might appear to be all right and give you a quarter or a half dollar or something, and then go right and give you away. White men will do that, but not a nigger. You can trust them. They are squarer with kids. I don't know why.

At the Saratoga meeting that year there were a lot of men from home. Dave Williams and Arthur Mulford and Merry Myers and others. Then there was a lot from Louisville and Lexington Henry Rieback knew but I didn't. They were professional gamblers and Henry Rieback's father is one too. He is what is called a sheet writer and goes away most of the year to tracks. In the winter when he is home in Beckersville he don't stay there much but goes away to cities and deals faro. He is a nice man and generous, is always sending Henry presents, a bicycle and a gold watch and a boy scout suit of clothes and things like that.

My own father is a lawyer. He's all right, but don't make much money and can't buy me things and anyway I'm getting so old now I don't expect it. He never said nothing to me against Henry, but Hanley Turner and Tom Tum-

berton's fathers did. They said to their boys that money
so come by is no good and they didn't want their boys
brought up to hear gamblers' talk and be thinking about
such things and maybe embrace them.

That's all right and I guess the men know what they are
talking about, but I don't see what it's got to do with
Henry or with horses either. That's what I'm writing this
story about. I'm puzzled. I'm getting to be a man and
want to think straight and be O.K., and there's something
I saw at the race meeting at the eastern track I can't figure
out.

I can't help it, I'm crazy about thoroughbred horses.
I've always been that way. When I was ten years old and
saw I was growing to be big and couldn't be a rider I was
so sorry I nearly died. Harry Hellinfinger in Beckersville,
whose father is Postmaster, is grown up and too lazy to
work, but likes to stand around in the street and get up
jokes on boys like sending them to a hardware store for a
gimlet to bore square holes and other jokes like that. He
played one on me. He told me that if I would eat a half a
cigar I would be stunted and not grow any more and
maybe could be a rider. I did it. When father wasn't
looking I took a cigar out of his pocket and gagged
it down some way. It made me awful sick and the doctor had to be sent for, and then it did no good. I kept
right on growing. It was a joke. When I told what I had
done and why most fathers would have whipped me but
mine didn't.

Well, I didn't get stunted and didn't die. It serves Harry
Hellinfinger right. Then I made up my mind I would like
to be a stable boy, but had to give that up too. Mostly
niggers do that work and I knew father wouldn't let me
go into it. No use to ask him.

If you've never been crazy about thoroughbreds it's

because you've never been around where they are much
and don't know any better. They're beautiful. There isn't
anything so lovely and clean and full of spunk and honest
and everything as some race horses. On the big horse
farms that are all around our town Beckersville there are
tracks and the horses run in the early morning. More
than a thousand times I've got out of bed before daylight
and walked two or three miles to the tracks. Mother
wouldn't of let me go but father always says, "Let him
alone," So I got some bread out of the bread box and
some butter and jam, gobbled it and lit out.

At the tracks you sit on the fence with men, whites and
niggers, and they chew tobacco and talk, and then the
colts are brought out. It's early and the grass is covered
with shiny dew and in another field a man is plowing and
they are frying things in a shed where the track niggers
sleep, and you know how a nigger can giggle and laugh
and say things that make you laugh. A white man can't do
it and some niggers can't but a track nigger can
every time.

And so the colts are brought out and some are just
galloped by stable boys, but almost every morning on a
big track owned by a rich man who lives maybe in New
York, there are always, nearly every morning, a few colts
and some of the old race horses and geldings and mares
that are cut loose.

It brings a lump up into my throat when a horse runs. I
don't mean all horses but some. I can pick them nearly
every time. It's in my blood like in the blood of race track
niggers and trainers. Even when they just go slop-jogging
along with a little nigger on their backs I can tell a winner.
If my throat hurts and it's hard for me to swallow, that's
him. He'll run like Sam Hill when you let him out. If he
don't win every time it'll be a wonder and because they've

got him in a pocket behind another or he was pulled or got off bad at the post or something. If I wanted to be a gambler like Henry Rieback's father I could get rich. I know I could and Henry says so too. All I would have to do is to wait 'til that hurt comes when I see a horse and then bet every cent. That's what I would do if I wanted to be a gambler, but I don't.

When you're at the tracks in the morning—not the race tracks but the training tracks around Beckersville—you don't see a horse, the kind I've been talking about, very often, but it's nice anyway. Any thoroughbred, that is sired right and out of a good mare and trained by a man that knows how, can run. If he couldn't what would he be there for and not pulling a plow?

Well, out of the stables they come and the boys are on their backs and it's lovely to be there. You hunch down on top of the fence and itch inside you. Over in the sheds the niggers giggle and sing. Bacon is being fried and coffee made. Everything smells lovely. Nothing smells better than coffee and manure and horses and niggers and bacon frying and pipes being smoked out of doors on a morning like that. It just gets you, that's what it does.

But about Saratoga. We was there six days and not a soul from home seen us and everything came off just as we wanted it to, fine weather and horses and races and all. We beat our way home and Bildad gave us a basket with fried chicken and bread and other eatables in, and I had eighteen dollars when we got back to Beckersville. Mother jawed and cried but Pop didn't say much. I told everything we done except one thing. I did and saw that alone. That's what I'm writing about. It got me upset. I think about it at night. Here it is.

At Saratoga we laid up nights in the hay in the shed Bildad had showed us and ate with the niggers early and at night when the race people had all gone away. The men from home stayed mostly in the grandstand and betting field, and didn't come out around the places where the horses are kept except to the paddocks just before a race when the horses are saddled. At Saratoga they don't have paddocks under an open shed as at Lexington and Churchill Downs and other tracks down in our country, but saddle the horses right out in an open place under trees on a lawn as smooth and nice as Banker Bohon's front yard here in Beckersville. It's lovely. The horses are sweaty and nervous and shine and the men come out and smoke cigars and look at them and the trainers are there and the owners, and your heart thumps so you can hardly breathe.

Then the bugle blows for post and the boys that ride come running out with their silk clothes on and you run to get a place by the fence with the niggers.

I always am wanting to be a trainer or owner, and at the risk of being seen and caught and sent home I went to the paddocks before every race. The other boys didn't but I did.

We got to Saratoga on a Friday and on Wednesday the next week the big Mullford Handicap was to be run. Middlestride was in it and Sunstreak. The weather was fine and the track fast. I couldn't sleep the night before.

What had happened was that both these horses are the kind it makes my throat hurt to see. Middlestride is long and looks awkward and is a gelding. He belongs to Joe Thompson, a little owner from home who only has a half dozen horses. The Mullford Handicap is for a mile and Middlestride can't untrack fast. He goes away slow and is always way back at the half, then he begins to run and if the race is a mile and a quarter he'll just eat up everything and get there.

Sunstreak is different. He is a stallion and nervous and belongs on the biggest farm we've got in our country, the Van Riddle place that belongs to Mr. Van Riddle of New York. Sunstreak is like a girl you think about sometimes but never see. He is hard all over and lovely too. When you look at his head you want to kiss him. He is trained by Jerry Tillford who knows me and has been good to me lots of times, lets me walk into a horse's stall to look at him close and other things. There isn't anything as sweet as that horse. He stands at the post quiet and not letting on, but he is just burning up inside. Then when the barrier goes up he is off like his name, Sunstreak. It makes you ache to see him. It hurts you. He just lays down and runs like a bird dog. There can't anything I ever see run like him except Middlestride when he gets untracked and stretches himself.

Gee! I ached to see that race and those two horses run, ached and dreaded it too. I didn't want to see either of our horses beaten. We had never sent a pair like that to the races before. Old men in Beckersville said so and the nigger said so. It was a fact.

Before the race I went over to the paddocks to see. I looked a last look at Middlestride, who isn't such a much standing in a paddock that way, then I went to see Sunstreak.

It was his day. I knew when I seen him. I forgot all about being seen myself and walked right up. All the men from Beckersville were there and no one noticed me except Jerry Tillford. He saw me and something happened. I'll tell you about that.

I was standing looking at that horse and aching. In some way, I can't tell how, I knew just how Sunstreak felt inside. He was quiet and letting the niggers rub his legs and Mr. Van Riddle himself put the saddle on, but he was just a raging torrent inside. He was like the water in the river at Niagara Falls just before it goes plunk down. That horse wasn't thinking about running. He don't have to think about that. He was just thinking about holding himself back 'til the time for the running came. I knew that. I could just in a way see right inside him. He was going to do some awful running and I knew it. He wasn't bragging or letting on much or prancing or making a fuss, but just waiting. I knew it and Jerry Tillford his trainer knew. I looked up and then that man and I looked into each other's eyes. Something happened to me. I guess I loved the man as much as I did the horse because he knew what I knew. Seemed to me there wasn't anything in the world but that man and the horse and me. I cried and Jerry Tillford had a shine in his eyes. Then I came away to the fence to wait for the race. The horse was better than me, more steadier, and now I know better than Jerry. He was the quietest and he had to do the running.

Sunstreak ran first of course and he busted the world's record for a mile. I've seen that if I never see anything more. Everything came out just as I expected. Middle-stride got left at the post and I was way back and closed up to be second, just as I knew he would. He'll get a world's record too some day. They can't skin the Beckersville country on horses.

I watched the race calm because I knew what would happen. I was sure. Hanley Turner and Henry Rieback and Tom Tumberton were all more excited than me.

A funny thing had happened to me. I was thinking about Jerry Tillford the trainer and how happy he was all through the race. I liked him that afternoon even more than I ever liked my own father. I almost forget the horses thinking that way about him. It was because of what I had seen in his eyes as he stood in the paddocks beside Sunstreak before the race started. I knew he had been watching and working with Sunstreak since the horse was a baby colt, had taught him to run and be patient and when to let himself out and not to quit, never. I knew that for him it was like a mother seeing her child do something brave or wonderful. It was the first time I ever felt for a man like that.

After the race that night I cut out from Tom and Hanley and Henry. I wanted to be by myself and I wanted to be near Jerry Tillford if I could work it. Here is what happened.

The track in Saratoga is near the edge of town. It is all polished up and trees around, the evergreen kind, and grass and everything painted and nice. If you go past the track you get to a hard road made of asphalt for automobiles, and if you go along this for a few miles there is a road turns off to a little rummy-looking farm house set in a yard.

That night after the race I went along that road because I had seen Jerry and some other men go that way in an automobile. I didn't expect to find them. I walked for a ways and then sat down by a fence to think. It was the direction they went in. I wanted to be as near Jerry as I could. I felt close to him. Pretty soon I went up the side road—I don't know why—and came to the rummy farm house. I was just lonesome to see Jerry, like wanting to see your father at night when you are a young kid. Just then an automobile came along and turned in. Jerry was in it and Henry Rieback's father, and Arthur Bedford from home, and Dave Williams and two other men I didn't know. They got out of the car and went into the house, all but Henry Rieback's father who quarreled with them and said he wouldn't go. It was only about nine o'clock, but they were all drunk and the rummy looking farm house was a place for bad women to stay in. That's what it was. I crept up along a fence and looked through a window and saw.

It's what gave me the fantods. I can't make it out. The women in the house were all ugly mean-looking women, not nice to look at or be near. They were homely too, except one who was tall and looked a little like the gelding Middlestride, but not clean like him, but with a hard ugly mouth. She had red hair. I saw everything plain. I got up by an old rose bush by an open window and looked. The women had on loose dresses and sat around in chairs. The men came in and some sat on the women's laps. The place smelled rotten and there was rotten talk, the kind a kid hears around a livery stable in a town like Beckersville in the winter but don't ever expect to hear talked when there are women around. It was rotten. A nigger wouldn't go into such a place.

I looked at Jerry Tillford. I've told you how I had been feeling about him on account of his knowing what was going on inside of Sunstreak in the minute before he went to the post for the race in which he made a world's record.

Jerry bragged in that bad woman house as I know Sunstreak wouldn't never have bragged. He said that he made that horse, that it was him that won the race and made the record. He lied and bragged like a fool. I never heard such silly talk.

And then, what do you suppose he did! He looked at the woman in there, the one that was lean and hard-mouthed and looked a little like the gelding Middle-stride, but not clean like him, and his eyes began to shine just as they did when he looked at me and at Sunstreak in the paddocks at the track in the afternoon. I stood there by the window—gee!—but I wished I hadn't gone away from the tracks, but had stayed with the boys and the niggers and the horses. The tall rotten looking woman was between us just as Sunstreak was in the paddocks in the afternoon.

Then, all of a sudden, I began to hate that man. I wanted to scream and rush in the room and kill him. I never had such a feeling before. I was so mad clean through that I cried and my fists were doubled up so my finger nails cut my hands.

And Jerry's eyes kept shining and he waved back and forth, and then he went and kissed that woman and I crept away and went back to the tracks and to bed and didn't sleep hardly any, and then next day I got the other kids to start home with me and never told them anything I seen.

I been thinking about it ever since. I can't make it out. Spring has come again and I'm nearly sixteen and go to the tracks mornings same as always, and I see Sunstreak and Middlestride and a new colt named Strident I'll bet will lay them all out, but no one thinks so but me and two or three niggers.

But things are different. At the tracks the air don't taste as good or smell as good. It's because a man like Jerry Tillford, who knows what he does, could see a horse like Sunstreak run, and kiss a woman like that the same day. I can't make it out. Darn him, what did he want to do like that for? I keep thinking about it and it spoils looking at horses and smelling things and hearing niggers laugh and everything. Sometimes I'm so mad about it I want to fight someone. It gives me the fantods. What did he do it for? I want to know why.

There She Is —
She Is Taking Her Bath

Another day when I have done no work. It is maddening. I went to the office this morning as usual and tonight came home at the regular time. My wife and I live in an apartment in the Bronx, here in New York City, and we have no children. I am ten years older than she. Our apartment is on the second floor and there is a little hallway downstairs used by all the people in the building.

If I could only decide whether or not I am a fool, a man turned suddenly a little mad or a man whose honor has really been tampered with, I should be quite all right. Tonight I went home, after something most unusual had happened at the office, determined to tell everything to my wife. "I will tell her and then watch her face. If she blanches, then I will know all I suspect is true," I said to myself. Within the last two weeks everything about me has changed. I am no longer the same man. For example, I never in my life before used the word "blanched." What does it mean? How am I to tell whether my wife blanches or not when I do not know what the word means? It must be a word I saw in a book when I was a boy, perhaps a book of detective stories. But wait, I know how that happened to pop into my head.

But that is not what I started to tell you about. Tonight, as I have already said, I came home and climbed the stairs to our apartment.

When I got inside the house I spoke in a loud voice to my wife. "My dear, what are you doing?" I asked. My voice sounded strange.

"I am taking a bath," my wife answered.

And so you see she was at home taking a bath. There she was.

She is always pretending she loves me, but look at her now. Am I in her thoughts? Is there a tender look in her eyes? Is she dreaming of me as she walks along the streets?

You see she is smiling. There is a young man who has just passed her. He is a tall fellow with a little mustache and is smoking a cigarette. Now I ask you—is he one of the men who, like myself, does, in a way, keep the world going?

Once I knew a man who was president of a whist club. Well, he was something. People wanted to know how to play whist. They wrote to him. "If it turns out that after three cards are played the man to my right still has three cards while I have only two, etc., etc."

My friend, the man of whom I am now speaking, looks the matter up. "In rule four hundred and six you will see, etc., etc.," he writes.

My point is that he is of some account in the world. He helps keep things going and I respect him. Often we used to have lunch together.

But I am a little off the point. The fellows of whom I am now thinking, these young squirts who go through the streets ogling women—what do they do? They twirl their mustaches. They carry canes. Some honest man is supporting them too. Some fool is their father.

And such a fellow is walking in the street. He meets a woman like my wife, an honest woman without too much experience of life. He smiles. A tender look comes into his eyes. Such deceit. Such callow nonsense.

And how are the women to know? They are children. They know nothing. There is a man, working somewhere in an office, keeping things moving, but do they think of him?

The truth is the woman is flattered. A tender look, that should be saved and bestowed only upon her husband, is thrown away. One never knows what will happen.

But pshaw, if I am to tell you the story, let me begin. There are men everywhere who talk and talk, saying nothing. I am afraid I am becoming one of that kind. As I have already told you, I have come home from the office at evening and am standing in the hallway of our apartment, just inside the door. I have asked my wife what she is doing and she has told me she is taking a bath.

Very well, I am then a fool. I shall go out for a walk in the park. There is no use my not facing everything frankly. By facing everything frankly one gets everything quite cleared up.

Aha! The very devil has got into me now. I said I would remain cool and collected, but I am not cool. The truth is I am growing angry.

I am a small man but I tell you that, once aroused, I will fight. Once when I was a boy I fought another boy in the school yard. He gave me a black eye but I loosened one of his teeth. "There, take that and that. Now I have got you against the wall. I will muss your mustache. Give me that cane. I will break it over your head. I do not intend to kill you, young man. I intend to vindicate my honor. No, I will not let you go. Take that and that. When next you see a respectable married woman on the street, going to the

store, behaving herself, do not look at her with a tender
light in your eyes. What you had better do is to go to
work. Get a job in a bank. Work your way up. You said I
was an old goat but I will show you an old goat can butt.
Take that and that."

Very well, you, who read, also think me a fool. You
laugh. You smile. Look at me. You are walking along here
in the park. You are leading a dog.

Where is your wife? What is she doing?

Well, suppose she is at home taking a bath. What is she
thinking? If she is dreaming, as she takes her bath, of
whom is she dreaming?

I will tell you what, you who go along leading that dog,
you may have no reason to suspect your wife, but you are
in the same position as myself.

She was at home taking a bath and all day I had been
sitting at my desk and thinking such thoughts. Under the
circumstances I would never have had the temerity to go
calmly off and take a bath. I admire my wife. Ha, ha. If
she is innocent I admire her, of course, as a husband
should, and if she is guilty I admire her even more. What
nerve, what insouciance. There is something noble,
something almost heroic in her attitude toward me, just
at this time.

With me this day is like every day now. Well, you see, I
have been sitting all day with my head in my hand thinking and thinking and while I have been doing that she has
been going about, leading her regular life.

She has got up in the morning and has had her breakfast sitting opposite her husband; that is, myself. Her
husband has gone off to his office. Now she is speaking to
our maid. She is going to the stores. She is sewing,
perhaps making new curtains for the windows of our
apartment.

There is the woman for you. Nero fiddled while Rome was burning. There was something of the woman in him.

A wife has been unfaithful to her husband. She has gone gayly off, let us say on the arm of a young blade. Who is he? He dances. He smokes cigarettes. When he is with his companions, his own kind of fellows, he laughs. "I have got me a woman," he says. "She is not very young but she is terrifically in love with me. It is very convenient." I have heard such fellows talk, in the smoking cars, on trains and in other places.

And there is the husband, a fellow like myself. Is he calm? Is he collected? Is he cool? His honor is perhaps being tampered with. He sits at his desk. He smokes a cigar. People come and go. He is thinking, thinking.

And what are his thoughts? They concern her. "Now she is still at home, in our apartment," he thinks. "Now she is walking along a street." What do you know of the secret life led by your wife? What do you know of her thoughts? Well, hello! You smoke a pipe. You put your hands in your pockets. For you, your life is all very well. You are gay and happy. "What does it matter, my wife is at home taking a bath," you are telling yourself. In your daily life you are, let us say, a useful man. You publish books, you run a store, you write advertisements. Sometimes you say to yourself, "I am lifting the burden off the shoulders of others." That makes you feel good. I sympathize with you. If you let me, or rather I should say, if we had met in the formal transactions of our regular occupations, I dare say we would be great friends. Well, we would have lunch together, not too often, but now and then. I would tell you of some real-estate deal and you would tell me what you had been doing. "I am glad we met! Call me up. Before you go away, have a cigar."

With me it is quite different. All today, for example, I

have been in my office, but I have not worked. A man came in, a Mr. Albright. "Well, are you going to let that property go or are you going to hold on?" he said.

What property did he mean? What was he talking about?

You can see for yourself what a state I am in.

And now I must be going home. My wife will have finished taking her bath. We will sit down to dinner. Nothing of all this I have been speaking about will be mentioned at all. "John, what is the matter with you?" "Aha. There is nothing the matter. I am worried about business a little. A Mr. Albright came in. Shall I sell or shall I hold on?" The real thing that is on my mind shall not be mentioned at all. I will grow a little nervous. The coffee will be spilled on the table-cloth or I will upset my dessert.

"John, what is the matter with you?" What coolness. As I have already said, what insouciance.

What is the matter? Matter enough.

A week, two weeks, to be exact, just seventeen days ago, I was a happy man. I went about my affairs. In the morning I rode to my office in the subway, but, had I wished to do so, I could long ago have bought an automobile.

But no, long ago, my wife and I had agreed there should be no such silly extravagance. To tell the truth, just ten years ago I failed in business and had to put some property in my wife's name. I bring the papers home to her and she signs. That is the way it is done.

"Well, John," said my wife, "we will not get us any automobile." That was before the thing happened that so upset me. We were walking together in the park. "Mabel, shall we get us an automobile?" I asked. "No," she said, "we will not get us an automobile." "Our money," she has said, more than a thousand times, "will be a comfort to us later."

A comfort indeed. What can be a comfort now that this thing has happened?

It was just two weeks, more than that, just seventeen days ago, that I went home from the office just as I came home tonight. Well, I walked in the same streets, passed the same stores.

I am puzzled as to what that Mr. Albright meant when he asked me if I intended to sell the property or hold on to it. I answered in a noncommittal way. "We'll see," I said To what property did he refer? We must have had some previous conversation regarding the matter. A mere acquaintance does not come into your office and speak of property in that careless, one might say, familiar way, without having previous conversation on the same subject.

As you see I am still a little confused. Even though I am facing things now, I am still, as you have guessed, somewhat confused. This morning I was in the bathroom, shaving as usual. I always shave in the morning, not in the evening, unless my wife and I are going out. I was shaving and my shaving brush dropped to the floor. I stooped to pick it up and struck my head on the bath-tub. I only tell you this to show what a state I am in. It made a large bump on my head. My wife heard me groan and asked me what was the matter. "I struck my head," I said. Of course, one quite in control of his faculties does not hit his head on a bath-tub when he knows it is there, and what man does not know where the bath-tub stands in his own house?

But now I am thinking again of what happened, of what has upset me this way. I was going home on that evening, just seventeen days ago. Well, I walked along, thinking nothing. When I reached our apartment build-

ing I went in, and there, lying on the floor in the little
hallway, in front, was a pink envelope with my wife's
name, Mabel Smith, written on it. I picked it up thinking,
"This is strange." It had perfume on it and there was no
address, just the name Mabel Smith, written in a bold
man's hand.

I quite automatically opened it and read.

Since I first met her, twelve years ago at a party at Mr.
Westley's house, there have never been any secrets between me and my wife; at least, until that moment in the
hallway seventeen days ago this evening, I had never
thought there were any secrets between us. I have always
opened her letters and she had always opened mine. I
think it should be that way between a man and his wife. I
know there are some who do not agree with me but what
I have always argued is I am right.

I went to the party with Harry Selfridge and afterward
took my wife home. I offered to get a cab. "Shall we have a
cab?" I asked her. "No," she said, "let's walk." She was the
daughter of a man in the furniture business and he has
died since. Every one thought he would leave her some
money but he didn't. It turned out he owed almost all he
was worth to a firm in Grand Rapids. Some would have
been upset, but I wasn't. "I married you for love, my
dear," I said to her on the night when her father died. We
were walking home from his house, also in the Bronx,
and it was raining a little, but we did not get very wet. "I
married you for love," I said, and I meant what I said.

But to return to the note. "Dear Mabel," it said, "come
to the park on Wednesday when the old goat has gone
away. Wait for me on the bench near the animal cages
where I met you before."

It was signed Bill. I put it in my pocket and went
upstairs.

When I got into my apartment, I heard a man's voice. The voice was urging something upon my wife. Did the voice change when I came in? I walked boldly into our front room where my wife sat facing a young man who sat in another chair. He was tall and had a little mustache.

The man was pretending to be trying to sell my wife a patent carpet-sweeper, but just the same, when I sat down in a chair in the corner and remained there, keeping silent, they both became self-conscious. My wife, in fact, became positively excited. She got up out of her chair and said in a loud voice, "I tell you I do not want any carpet-sweeper."

The young man got up and went to the door and I followed. "Well, I had better be getting out of here," he was saying to himself. And so he had been intending to leave a note telling my wife to meet him in the park on Wednesday but at the last moment he had decided to take the risk of coming to our house. What he had probably thought was something like this: "Her husband may come and get the note out of the mail box." Then he decided to come and see her and had quite accidentally dropped the note in the hallway. Now he was frightened. One could see that. Such men as myself are small but we will fight sometimes.

He hurried to the door and I followed him into the hallway. There was another young man coming from the floor above, also with a carpet-sweeper in his hand. It is a pretty sick scheme, this carrying carpet-sweepers with them, the young men of this generation have worked out, but we older men are not to have the wool pulled over our eyes. I saw through everything at once. The second young man was a confederate and had been concealed in the hallway in order to warn the first young man of my approach. When I got upstairs, of course, the first young man was pretending to sell my wife a carpet-sweeper. Perhaps the second young man had tapped with the handle of the carpet-sweeper on the floor above. Now that I think of that I remember there was a tapping sound.

At the time, however, I did not think everything out as I have since done. I stood in the hallway with my back against the wall and watched them go down the stairs. One of them turned and laughed at me, but I did not say anything. I suppose I might have gone down the stairs after them and challenged them both to fight but what I thought was, "I won't."

And sure enough, just as I suspected from the first, it was the young man pretending to sell carpet-sweepers I had found sitting in my apartment with my wife, who had lost the note. When they got down to the hallway at the front of the house the man I had caught with my wife began to feel in his pocket. Then, as I leaned over the railing above, I saw him looking about the hallway. He laughed. "Say, Tom, I had a note to Mabel in my pocket. I intended to get a stamp at the postoffice and mail it. I had forgotten the street number. 'Oh, well,' I thought, 'I'll go see her!' I didn't want to bump into that old goat, her husband."

"You have bumped into him," I said to myself; "now we will see who will come out victorious."

I went into our apartment and closed the door.

For a long time, perhaps for ten minutes, I stood just inside the door of our apartment thinking and thinking, just as I have been doing ever since. Two or three times I tried to speak, to call out to my wife, to question her and find out the bitter truth at once but my voice failed me.

What was I to do? Was I to go to her, seize her by the wrists, force her down into a chair, make her confess at the risk of personal violence? I asked myself that question.

"No," I said to myself, "I will not do that. I will use finesse."

For a long time I stood there thinking. My world had tumbled down about my ears. When I tried to speak, the words would not come out of my mouth.

At last I did speak, quite calmly. There is something of the man of the world about me. When I am compelled to meet a situation I do it. "What are you doing?" I said to my wife, speaking in a calm voice. "I am taking a bath," she answered.

And so I left the house and came out here to the park to think, just as I have done tonight. On that night, and just as I came out at our front door, I did something I have not done since I was a boy. I am a deeply religious man but I swore. My wife and I have had a good many arguments as to whether or not a man in business should have dealings with those who do such things; that is to say, with men who swear. "I cannot refuse to sell a man a piece of property because he swears," I have always said. "Yes, you can," my wife says.

It only shows how little women know about business. What I have always maintained is I am right.

And I maintain too that we men must protect the integrity of our homes and our firesides. On that first night I walked about until dinner time and then went home. I had decided not to say anything for the present but to remain quiet and use finesse, but at dinner my hand trembled and I spilled the dessert on the tablecloth.

And a week later I went to see a detective.

But first something else happened. On Wednesday—I had found the note on Monday evening — I could not bear sitting in my office and thinking perhaps that that young squirt was meeting my wife in the park, so I went to the park myself.

Sure enough there was my wife sitting on a bench near the animal cages and knitting a sweater.

At first I thought I would conceal myself in some bushes but instead I went to where she was seated and sat down beside her. "How nice! What brings you here?" my wife said smiling. She looked at me with surprise in her eyes.

Was I to tell her or was I not to tell her? It was a moot question with me. "No," I said to myself. "I will not. I will go see a detective. My honor has no doubt already been tampered with and I shall find out." My naturally quick wits came to my rescue. Looking directly into my wife's eyes I said: "There was a paper to be signed and I had my own reasons for thinking you might be here, in the park."

As soon as I had spoken I could have torn out my tongue. However, she had noticed nothing and I took a paper out of my pocket and, handing her my fountain pen, asked her to sign; and when she had done so I hurried away. At first I thought perhaps I would linger about, in the distance, that is to say, but no, I decided not to do that. He will no doubt have his confederate on the watchout for me, I told myself.

And so on the next afternoon, I went to the office of the detective. He was a large man, and when I told him what I wanted he smiled. "I understand," he said, "we have many such cases. We'll track the guy down."

And so, you see, there it was. Everything was arranged. It was to cost me a pretty penny but my house was to be watched and I was to have a report on everything. To tell the truth, when everything was arranged I felt ashamed of myself. The man in the detective place — there were several men standing about — followed me to the door and put his hand on my shoulder. For some reason I don't understand, that made me mad. He kept patting me on the shoulder as though I were a little boy. "Don't worry. We'll manage everything," was what he said. It was all right. Business is business but for some reason I wanted to bang him in the face with my fist.

That's the way I am, you see. I can't make myself out. "Am I a fool, or am I a man among men?" I keep asking myself, and I can't get an answer.

After I had arranged with the detective I went home and didn't sleep all night long.

To tell the truth I began to wish I had never found that note. I suppose that is wrong of me. It makes me less a man, perhaps, but it's the truth.

Well, you see, I couldn't sleep. "No matter what my wife was up to I could sleep now if I hadn't found that note," was what I said to myself. It was dreadful. I was ashamed of what I had done and at the same time ashamed of myself for being ashamed. I had done what any American man, who is a man at all, would have done, and there I was. I couldn't sleep. Every time I came home in the evening I kept thinking: "There is that man standing over there by a tree—I'll bet he is a detective." I kept thinking of the fellow who had patted me on the shoulders in the detective office, and every time I thought of him I grew madder and madder. Pretty soon I hated him more than I did the young man who had pretended to sell the carpet-sweeper to Mabel.

And then I did the most foolish thing of all. One afternoon—it was just a week ago—I thought of something. When I had been in the detective office I had seen several men standing about but had not been introduced to any of them. "And so," I thought, "I'll go there pretending to get my reports. If the man I engaged is not there I'll engage some one else."

So I did it. I went to the detective office, and sure enough my man was out. There was another fellow sitting by a desk and I made a sign to him. We went into an inner office. "Look here," I whispered; you see I had made up my mind to pretend I was the man who was ruining my own fireside, wrecking my own honor. "Do I make clear what I mean?"

It was like this, you see—well, I had to have some sleep, didn't I? Only the night before my wife had said to me, "John, I think you had better run away for a little vacation. Run away by yourself for a time and forget about business."

At another time her saying that would have been nice, you see, but now it only upset me worse than ever. "She wants me out of the way," I thought, and for just a moment I felt like jumping up and telling her everything I knew. Still I didn't. "I'll just keep quiet. I'll use finesse," I thought.

A pretty kind of finesse. There I was in that detective office again hiring a second detective. I came right out and pretended I was my wife's paramour. The man kept nodding his head and I kept whispering like a fool. Well, I told him that a man named Smith had hired a detective from that office to watch his wife. "I have my own reasons for wanting him to get a report that his wife is all right," I said, pushing some money across a table toward him. I had become utterly reckless about money. "Here is fifty dollars and when he gets such a report from your office you come to me and you may have two hundred more," I said.

I had thought everything out. I told the second man my name was Jones and that I worked in the same office with Smith. "I'm in business with him," I said, "a silent partner, you see."

Then I went out and, of course, he, like the first one, followed me to the door and patted me on the shoulder. That was the hardest thing of all to stand, but I stood it. A man has to have sleep.

And, of course, today both men had to come to my office within five minutes of each other. The first one came, of course, and told me my wife was innocent. "She is as innocent as a little lamb," he said. "I congratulate you upon having such an innocent wife."

Then I paid him, backing away so he couldn't pat me on the shoulders, and he had only just closed the door when in came the other man, asking for Jones.

And I had to see him too and give him two hundred dollars.

Then I decided to come on home, and I did, walking along the same street I have walked on every afternoon since my wife and I married. I went home and climbed the stairs to our apartment just as I described everything to you a little while ago. I could not decide whether I was a fool, a man who has gone a little mad, or a man whose honor has been tampered with, but anyway I knew there would be no detectives about.

What I thought was that I would go home and have eerything out with my wife, tell her of my suspicions and then watch her face. As I have said before, I intended to watch her face and see if she blanched when I told her of the note I had found in the hallway donstairs. The word "blanched" got into my mind because I once read it in a detective story when I was a boy and I had been dealing with detectives.

And so I intended to face my wife down, force a confession from her, but you see how it turned out. When I got home the apartment was silent and at first I thought it was empty. "Has she run away with him?" I asked myself, and maybe my own face blanched a little.

"Where are you, dear, what are you doing?"

I shouted in a loud voice and she told me she was taking a bath.

And so I came out here in the park.

But now I must be going home. Dinner will be waiting. I am wondering what property that Mr. Allbright had in his mind. When I sit at dinner with my wife my hands will shake. I will spill the dessert. A man does not come in and speak of property in that offhand manner unless there has been conversation about it before.

Another Wife

He thought himself compelled to say something special to her — knowing her — loving her — wanting her. What he thought was that perhaps she wanted him too, or she wouldn't have spent so much time with him. He wasn't exactly modest.

After all, he was modest enough. He was quite sure several men must have loved her and thought it not unlikely she had experimented with at least a few of them. It was all imagined. Seeing her about had started his mind — his thoughts — racing. "Modern women, of her class, used to luxuries, sensitive, are not going to miss anything, even though they don't take the final plunge into matrimony as I did when I was younger," he thought. The notion of sin had, for him, more or less been taken out of that sort of thing. "What you try to do, if you are a modern woman with any class to you, is to try to use your head," he thought.

He was forty-seven and she ten years younger. His wife had been dead two years.

For the last month she had been in the habit of coming down from her mother's country house to his cabin two or three evenings a week. She might have invited him up the hill to the house — would have invited him oftener —

but that she preferred having him, his society, in his own cabin. The family, her family, had simply left the whole matter to her, let her manage it. She lived in her mother's country house, with the mother and two younger sisters — both unmarried. They were delightful people to be with. It was the first summer he had been up in that country and he had met them after he took the cabin. He ate at a hotel nearly a half mile away. Dinner was served early. By getting right back he could be sure of being at home if she decided to stroll down his way.

Being with her, at her mother's house with the others, was fun, of course, but some one was always dropping in. He thought the sisters liked to tease her and him by arranging things that would tie them down.

It was all pure fancy, just a notion. Why should they be concerned about him?

What a whirlpool of notions were stirred up in him that Summer by the woman! He thought about her all the time, having really nothing else to do. Well, he had come to the country to rest. His one son was at a Summer school.

"It's like this — here I am, practically alone. What am I letting myself in for? If she, if any of the women of that family, were of the marrying sort, she would have made a marriage with a much more likely man long ago." Her younger sisters were so considerate in their attitude toward her. There was something tender, respectful, teasing, too, about the way they acted when he and she were together.

Little thoughts kept running through his head. He had come to the country because something inside him had let down. It might have been his forty-seven years. A man like himself, who had begun life as a poor boy, worked himself up in his profession, who had become a physician of some note—well, a man dreams his dreams, he wants a lot.

At forty-seven he is likely, at any moment, to run into a slump.

You won't get half, a third of what you wanted, in your work, in life. What's the use going on? These older men who keep on striving like young men, what about them? They are a little childlike, immature, really.

A great man might go on like that, to the bitter end, to the brink of the grave, but who, having any sense, any head, wants to be a great man? What is called a great man may be just an illusion in people's minds. Who wants to be an illusion?

Thoughts like that, driving him out of the city—to rest. God knows it would have been a mistake if she hadn't been there. Before he met her and before she got into the unwomanly habit of coming to see him in his own cabin during the long Summer evenings, the country, the quiet of the country, was dreadful.

"It may be she only comes down here to me because she is bored. A woman like that, who has known many men, brilliant men, who has been loved by men of note. Still, why does she come? I'm not so gay. It's sure she doesn't think me witty or brilliant."

She was thirty-seven, a bit inclined to extremes in dress, plump, to say the least. Life didn't seem to have quieted her much.

When she came down to his cabin, at the edge of the stream facing the country road, she dropped onto a couch by the door and lit a cigarette. She had lovely ankles. Really, they were beautiful ankles.

The door was open and he sat by a chair near a table. He burned an oil-lamp. The cabin door was left open.

Country people went past.

"The trouble with all this silly business about resting is that a man thinks too much. A physician in practice — people coming in, other people's troubles—hasn't time."

Woman had come to him a good deal — married and unmarried women. One woman — she was married — wrote him a long letter after he had been treating her for three years. She had gone with her husband to California. "Now that I am away from you, will not see you again, I tell you frankly I love you."

What an idea!

"You have been patient with me for these three years, have let me talk to you. I have told you all the intimate things of my life. You have been always a little aloof and wise."

What nonsense! How could he have stopped the woman's talking intimately? There was more of that sort of thing in the letter. The doctor did not feel he had been specially wise with the woman patient. He had really been afraid of her. What she had thought was aloofness was really fright.

Still, he had kept the letter—for a time. He destroyed it finally because he did not want it to fall accidentally into his wife's hands.

A man likes to feel he has been of some account to some one.

The doctor, say, in the cabin, the new woman near him. She was smoking a cigarette. It was Saturday evening. People—men, women and children—were going along the country road toward a mountain town. Presently the country women and children would be coming back without the men. On Saturday evenings nearly all the mountain-men got drunk.

You come from the city and, because the hills are

green, the water in mountain streams clear, you think the people of the hills must be at the bottom clear and sweet.

Now the country people in the road were turning to stare into the cabin at the woman and the doctor. On a previous Saturday evening, after midnight, the doctor had been awakened by a noisy drunken conversation carried on in the road. It had made him tremble with wrath. He had wanted to rush out into the road and fight the drunken country men, but a man of forty-seven ... The men in the road were sturdy young fellows.

One of the men was telling the others in a loud voice that the woman now on the couch near the doctor—that she was really a loose city woman. He had used a very distasteful word and had sworn to the others that, before the Summer was over, he intended having her himself.

It was just crude drunken talk. The fellow had laughed when he said it, and the others had laughed. It was a drunken man trying to be funny.

If the woman with the doctor had known—if he told her? She would only have smiled.

How many thoughts about her in the doctor's head! He felt sure she had never cared much what others thought. They had been sitting like that, she smoking her after-dinner cigarette, he thinking, but a few minutes. In her presence, thoughts came quickly, dancing through his head. He wasn't used to such a multitude of thoughts. When he was in town—in practice—there were plenty of things to think of other than women, being in love with some woman.

With his wife it had never been like that. She had never excited him, except at first physically. After that he had just accepted her. "There are many woman. She is my woman. She is rather nice, does her share of the job" — that sort of an attitude.

When she had died it had left a gaping hole in his life. "That may be what is the matter with me."

"This other woman is a different sort surely. The way she dresses; her ease with people. Such people, having money always, from the first, a secure position in life — they just go along, quite sure of themselves, never afraid."

His early poverty had, the doctor thought, taught him a good many things he was glad to know. It had taught him other things not so good to know. Both he and his wife had always been a little afraid of people — of what people might think—of his standing in his profession. He had married a woman who also came from a poor family. She was a nurse before she married him. The woman now in the room with him got up from the couch and threw the end of her cigarette into the fireplace. "Let's walk," she said.

When they go out into the road and had turned away from the town and her mother's house, standing on a hill between his cabin and town, another person on the road behind might have thought him the distinguished one. She was a bit too plump—not tall enough—while he had a tall, rather slender figure and walked with a free, easy carriage. He carried his hat in his hand. His thick graying hairs added to his air of distinction.

The road grew more uneven and they walked close to each other. She was trying to tell him something. There had been something he had determined to tell her — on this very evening. What was it?

Something of what the woman in California had tried to tell him in that foolish letter—not doing very well at it — something to the effect that she — this new woman — met while he was off guard, resting — was aloof from himself—unattainable—but that he found himself in love with her.

If she found, by any odd chance, that she wanted him, then he would try to tell her.

After all, it was foolish. More thoughts in the doctor's head. "I can't be very ardent. This being in the country—resting—away from my practice—is all foolishness. My practice is in the hands of another man. There are cases a new man can't understand.

"My wife who died—she didn't expect much. She had been a nurse, was brought up in a poor family, had always had to work, while this new woman ... "

There had been some kind of nonsense the doctor had thought he might try to put into words. Then he would get back to town, back to his work. "I'd much better light out now, saying nothing."

She was telling him something about herself. It was about a man she had known and loved, perhaps.

Where had he got the notion she had had several lovers? He had merely thought—well, that sort of woman — always plenty of money — being always with clever people.

When she was younger she had thought for a time she would be a painter, had studied in New York and Paris.

She was telling him about an Englishman—a novelist.

The devil—how had she known his thoughts?

She was scolding him. What had he said?

She was talking about such people as himself, simple, straight, good people, she called them, people who go ahead in life, doing their work, not asking much.

She, then, had illusions as he had.

"Such people as you get such ideas in your heads—silly notions."

Now she was talking about herself again.

"I tried to be a painter. I had such ideas about the so-called big men in the arts. You, being a doctor, without a great reputation—I have no doubt you have all sorts of ideas about so-called great doctors, great surgeons."

Now she was telling what happened to her. There had been an English novelist she had met in Paris. He had an established reputation. When he seemed attracted to her she had been much excited.

The novelist had written a love story and she had read it. It had just a certain tone. She had always thought that above everything in life she wanted a love affair in just that tone. She had tried it with the writer of the story and it had turned out nothing of the sort.

It was growing dark in the road. Laurels and elders grew on a hillside. In the half-darkness he could see faintly the little hurt shrug of her shoulders.

Had all the lovers he had imagined for her, the brilliant, witty men of the great world, been like that? He felt suddenly as he had felt when the drunken country men talked in the road. He wanted to hit someone with his fist, in particular he wanted to hit a novelist—preferably an English novelist—or a painter or musician.

He had never known any such people. There weren't any about. He smiled at himself, thinking: "When that country man talked I sat still and let him." His practice had been with well-to-do merchants, lawyers, manufacturers, their wives and families.

Now his body was trembling. They had come to a small bridge over a stream, and suddenly, without premeditation, he put his arm about her.

There had been something he had planned to tell her. What was it? It was something about himself. "I am no longer young. What I could have to offer you would not be much. I cannot offer it to such a one as yourself, to one who has known great people, been loved by witty, brilliant men."

There had no doubt been something of the sort he had foolishly thought of saying. Now she was in his arms in the darkness on the bridge. The air was heavy with Summer perfumes. She was a little heavy — a real armful. Evidently she liked having him hold her thus. He had thought, really, she might like him but have at the same time a kind of contempt for him.

Now he had kissed her. She liked that too. She moved closer and returned the kiss. He leaned over the bridge. It was a good thing there was a support of some sort. She was sturdily built. His first wife, after thirty, had been fairly plump, but this new woman weighed more.

And now they were again walking in the road. It was the most amazing thing. There was something quite taken for granted. It was that he wanted her to marry him.

Did he? They walked along the road toward his cabin and there was in him the half-foolish, half-joyful mood a boy feels walking in the darkness the first time, alone with a girl.

A quick rush of memories, evenings as a boy and as a young man remembered.

Does a man ever get too old for that? A man like himself, a physician, should know more about things. He was smiling at himself in the darkness — feeling foolish, feeling frightened, glad. Nothing definite had been said.

It was better at the cabin. How nice it had been of her to have no foolish, conventional fears about coming to see him! She was a nice person. Sitting alone with her in the darkness of the cabin he realized that they were at any rate both mature—grown up enough to know what they were doing.

Did they?

When they had returned to the cabin it was quite dark and he lighted an oil-lamp. It all got very definite very rapidly. She had another cigarette and sat as before, looking at him. Her eyes were gray. They were gray, wise eyes.

She was realizing perfectly his discomfiture. The eyes were smiling—being old eyes. The eyes were saying: "A man is a man and a woman is a woman. You can never tell how or when it will happen. You are a man and, although you think yourself a practical, unimaginative man, you are a good deal of a boy. There is a way in which any woman is older than any man and that is the reason I know."

Never mind what her eyes were saying. The doctor was plainly fussed. There had been a kind of speech he had intended making. It may have been he had known, from the first, that he was caught.

"O Lord, I won't get it in now."

He tried, haltingly, to say something about the life of a physician's wife. That he had assumed she might marry him, without asking her directly, seemed a bit rash. He was assuming it without intending anything of the sort. Everything was muddled.

The life of a physician's wife—a man like himself—in general practice—wasn't such a pleasant one. When he had started out as a physician he had really thought, some time, he might get into a great position, be some kind of a specialist.

But now—

Her eyes kept on smiling. If he was muddled she evidently wasn't. "There is something definite and solid about some women. They seem to know just what they want," he thought.

She wanted him.

What she said wasn't much. "Don't be so foolish. I've waited a long time for just you."

That was all. It was final, absolute—terribly disconcerting too. He went and kissed her, awkwardly. Now she had the air that had from the first disconcerted him, the air of worldliness. It might not be anything but her way of smoking a cigarette — an undoubtedly good, although rather bold, taste in clothes.

His other wife never seemed to think about clothes. She hadn't the knack.

Well, he had managed again to get her out of his cabin. It might be she had managed. His first wife had been a nurse before he married her. It might be that women who have been nurses should not marry physicians. They have too much respect for physicians, are taught to have too much respect. This one, he was quite sure, would never have too much respect.

It was all, when the doctor let it sink in, rather nice. He had taken the great leap and seemed suddenly to feel solid ground under his feet. How easy it had been!

They were walking along the road toward her mother's house. It was dark and he could not see her eyes.

He was thinking—

"Four women in her family. A new woman to be the mother of my son." Her mother was old and quiet and had sharp gray eyes. One of the younger sisters was a bit boyish. The other one—she was the handsome one of the family — sang Negro songs.

They had plenty of money. When it came to that his own income was quite adequate.

It would be nice, being a kind of older brother to the sisters, a son to her mother. O Lord!

They got to the gate before her mother's house and she let him kiss her again. Her lips were warm, her breath fragrant. He stood, still embarrassed, while she went up a path to the door. There was a light on the porch.

There was no doubt she was plump, solidly built. What absurd notions he had had!

Well, it was time to go on back to his cabin. He felt foolishly young, silly, afraid, glad.

"O Lord—I've got me a wife, another wife, a new one," he said to himself as he went along the road in the darkness. How glad and foolish and frightened he still felt! Would he get over it after a time?

The Other Woman

"I am in love with my wife," he said—a superfluous remark, as I had not questioned his attachment to the woman he had married. We walked for ten minutes and then he said it again. I turned to look at him. He began to talk and told me the tale I am now about to set down.

The thing he had on his mind happened during what must have been the most eventful week of his life. He was to be married on Friday afternoon. On Friday of the week before he got a telegram announcing his appointment to a government position. Something else happened that made him very proud and glad. In secret he was in the habit of writing verses and during the year before several of them had been printed in poetry magazines. One of the societies that give prizes for what they think the best poems published during the year put his name at the head of its list. The story of his triumph was printed in the newspapers of his home city and one of them also printed his picture.

As might have been expected he was excited and in a rather highly strung nervous state all during that week. Almost every evening he went to call on his fiancée, the daughter of a judge. When he got there the house was filled with people and many letters, telegrams and packages were being received. He stood a little to one side and men and women kept coming up to speak to him. They congratulated him upon his success in getting the government position and on his achievement as a poet. Everyone seemed to be praising him and when he went home and to bed he could not sleep. On Wednesday evening he went to the theatre and it seemed to him that people all over the house recognized him. Everyone nodded and smiled. After the first act five or six men and two women left their seats to gather about him. A little group was formed. Strangers sitting along the same row of seats stretched their necks and looked. He had never received so much attention before, and now a fever of expectancy took possession of him.

As he explained when he told me of his experience, it was for him an altogether abnormal time. He felt like one floating in air. When he got into bed after seeing so many people and hearing so many words of praise his head whirled round and round. When he closed his eyes a crowd of people invaded his room. It seemed as though the minds of all the people of his city were centred on himself. The most absurd fancies took possession of him. He imagined himself riding in a carriage through the streets of a city. Windows were thrown open and people ran out at the doors of houses. "There he is. That's him," they shouted, and at the words a glad cry arose. The carriage drove into a street blocked with people. A hundred thousand pairs of eyes looked up at him. "There you are! What a fellow you have managed to make of yourself!" the eyes seemed to be saying.

My friend could not explain whether the excitement of the people was due to the fact that he had written a new poem or whether, in his new government position, he had performed some notable act. The apartment where he lived at that time was on a street perched along the top of a cliff far out at the edge of his city, and from his bedroom window he could look down over trees and factory roofs to a river. As he could not sleep and as the fancies that kept crowding in upon him only made him more excited, he got out of bed and tried to think.

As would be natural under such circumstances, he tried to control his thoughts, but when he sat by the window and was wide awake a most unexpected and humiliating thing happened. The night was clear and fine. There was a moon. He wanted to dream of the woman who was to be his wife, to think out lines for noble poems or make plans that would affect his career. Much to his surprise his mind refused to do anything of the sort.

At a corner of the street where he lived there was a small cigar store and newspaper stand run by a fat man of forty and his wife, a small active woman with bright grey eyes. In the morning he stopped there to buy a paper before going down to the city. Sometimes he saw only the fat man, but often the man had disappeared and the woman waited on him. She was, as he assured me at least twenty times in telling me his tale, a very ordinary person with nothing special or notable about her, but for some reason he could not explain, being in her presence stirred him profoundly. During that week in the midst of his distraction she was the only person he knew who stood out clear and distinct in his mind. When he wanted so much to think noble thoughts he could think only of her. Before he knew what was happening his imagination had taken hold of the notion of having a love affair with the woman.

"I could not understand myself," he declared, in telling me the story. "At night, when the city was quiet and when

I should have been asleep, I thought about her all the time. After two or three days of that sort of thing the consciousness of her got into my daytime thoughts. I was terribly muddled. When I went to see the woman who is now my wife I found that my love for her was in no way affected by my vagrant thoughts. There was but one woman in the world I wanted to live with and to be my comrade in undertaking to improve my own character and my position in the world, but for the moment, you see, I wanted this other woman to be in my arms. She had worked her way into my being. On all sides people were saying I was a big man who would do big things, and there I was. That evening when I went to the theatre I walked home because I knew I would be unable to sleep, and to satisfy the annoying impulse in myself I went and stood on the sidewalk before the tobacco shop. It was a two story building, and I knew the woman lived upstairs with her husband. For a long time I stood in the darkness with my body pressed against the wall of the building, and then I thought of the two of them up there and no doubt in bed together. That made me furious.

"Then I grew more furious with myself. I went home and got into bed, shaken with anger. There are certain books of verse and some prose writings that have always moved me deeply, and so I put several books on a table by my bed.

"The voices in the books were like the voices of the dead. I did not hear them. The printed words would not penetrate into my consciousness. I tried to think of the woman I loved, but her figure had also become something far away, something with which I for the moment seemed to have nothing to do. I rolled and tumbled about in the bed. It was a miserable experience.

"On Thursday morning I went into the store. There

stood the woman alone. I think she knew how I felt. Perhaps she had been thinking of me as I had been thinking of her. A doubtful hesitating smile played about the corners of her mouth. She had on a dress made of cheap cloth and there was a tear on the shoulder. She must have been ten years older than myself. When I tried to put my pennies on the glass counter, behind which she stood, my hand trembled so that the pennies made a sharp rattling noise. When I spoke the voice that came out of my throat did not sound like anything that had ever belonged to me. It barely arose above a thick whisper. 'I want you,' I said. 'I want you very much. Can't you run away from your husband? Come to me at my apartment at seven tonight.'

"The woman did come to my apartment at seven. That morning she didn't say anything at all. For a minute perhaps we stood looking at each other. I had forgotten everything in the world but just her. Then she nodded her head and I went away. Now that I think of it I cannot remember a word I ever heard her say. She came to my apartment at seven and it was dark. You must understand this was in the month of October. I had not lighted a light and I had sent my servant away.

"During that day I was no good at all. Several men came to see me at my office, but I got all muddled up in trying to talk with them. They attributed my rattle-headedness to my approaching marriage and went away laughing.

"It was on that morning, just the day before my marriage, that I got a long and very beautiful letter from my fiancée. During the night before she also had been unable to sleep and had got out of bed to write the letter. Everything she said in it was very sharp and real, but she herself, as a living thing, seemed to have receded into the distance. It seemed to me that she was like a bird, flying far away in distant skies, and that I was like a perplexed bare-footed boy standing in the dusty road before a farm house and looking at her receding figure. I wonder if you will understand what I mean?

"In regard to the letter. In it she, the awakening woman, poured out her heart. She of course knew nothing of life, but she was a woman. She lay, I suppose, in her bed feeling nervous and wrought up as I had been doing. She realized that a great change was about to take place in her life and was glad and afraid too. There she lay thinking of it all. Then she got out of bed and began talking to me on the bit of paper. She told me how afraid she was and how glad too. Like most young women she had heard things whispered. In the letter she was very sweet and fine. 'For a long time, after we are married, we will forget we are a man and woman,' she wrote. 'We will be human beings. You must remember that I am ignorant and often I will be very stupid. You must love me and be very patient and kind. When I know more, when after a long time you have taught me the way of life, I will try to repay you. I will love you tenderly and passionately. The possibility of that is in me or I would not want to marry at all. I am afraid but I am also happy. O, I am so glad our marriage time is near at hand!'

"Now you see clearly enough what a mess I was in. In my office, after I had read my fiancée's letter, I became at once very resolute and strong. I remember that I got out of my chair and walked about, proud of the fact that I was to be the husband of so noble a woman. Right away I felt concerning her as I had been feeling about myself before I found out what a weak thing I was. To be sure I took a strong resolution that I would not be weak. At nine that evening I had planned to run in to see my fiancée. 'I'm all right now,' I said to myself. 'The beauty of her character has saved me from myself. I will go home now and send the other woman away.' In the morning I had telephoned to my servant and told him that I did not want him to be at the apartment that evening and I now picked up the telephone to tell him to stay at home.

"Then a thought came to me. 'I will not want him there in any event,' I told myself. 'What will he think when he sees a woman coming in my place on the evening before the day I am to be married?' I put the telephone down and prepared to go home. 'If I want my servant out of the apartment it is because I do not want him to hear me talk with the woman. I cannot be rude to her. I will have to make some kind of an explanation,' I said to myself.

"The woman came at seven o'clock, and, as you may have guessed, I let her in and forgot the resolution I had made. It is likely I never had any intention of doing anything else. There was a bell on my door, but she did not ring, but knocked very softly. It seems to me that everything she did that evening was soft and quiet, but very determined and quick. Do I make myself clear? When she came I was standing just within the door where I had been standing and waiting for a half hour. My hands were trembling as they had trembled in the morning when her eyes looked at me and when I tried to put the pennies on the counter in the store. When I opened the door she stepped quickly in and I took her into my arms. We stood together in the darkness. My hands no longer trembled. I felt very happy and strong.

"Although I have tried to make everything clear I have not told you what the woman I married is like. I have emphasized, you see, the other woman. I make the blind statement that I love my wife, and to a man of your shrewdness that means nothing at all. To tell the truth, had I not started to speak of this matter I would feel more comfortable. It is inevitable that I give you the impression that I am in love with the tobacconist's wife. That's not true. To be sure I was very conscious of her all during the week before my marriage, but after she had come to me at my apartment she went entirely out of my mind.

"Am I telling the truth? I am trying very hard to tell what happened to me. I am saying that I have not since that evening thought of the woman who came to my apartment. Now, to tell the facts of the case, that is not true. On that evening I went to my fiancée at nine, as she had asked me to do in her letter. In a kind of way I cannot explain the other woman went with me. This is what I mean — you see I had been thinking that if anything happened between me and the tobacconist's wife I would not be able to go through with my marriage. 'It is one thing or the other with me,' I had said to myself.

"As a matter of fact I went to see my beloved on that evening filled with a new faith in the outcome of our life together. I am afraid I muddle this matter in trying to tell it. A moment ago I said the other woman, the tobacconist's wife, went with me. I do not mean she went in fact. What I am trying to say is that something of her faith in her own desires and her courage in seeing things though went with me. Is that clear to you? When I got to my fiancée's house there was a crowd of people standing about. Some were relatives from distant places I had not seen before. She looked up quickly when I came into the room. My face must have been radiant. I never saw her so moved. She thought her letter had affected me deeply, and of course it had. Up she jumped and ran to meet me. She was like a glad child. Right before the people who turned and looked inquiringly at us, she said the thing that was in her mind. 'O, I am so happy,' she cried. 'You have understood. We will be two human beings. We will not have to be husband and wife.'

"As you may suppose everyone laughed, but I did not laugh. The tears came into my eyes. I was so happy I wanted to shout. Perhaps you understand what I mean. In the office that day when I read the letter my fiancée had written I had said to myself, 'I will take care of the dear little woman.' There was something smug, you see, about that. In her house when she cried out in that way, and when everyone laughed, what I said to myself was something like this: 'We will take care of ourselves.' I whispered something of the sort into her ears. To tell you the truth I had come down off my perch. The spirit of the other woman did that to me. Before all the people gathered about I held my fiancée close and we kissed. They thought it very sweet of us to be so affected at the sight of each other. What they would have thought had they known the truth about me God only knows!

"Twice now I have said that after that evening I never thought of the other woman at all. That is partially true but, sometimes in the evening when I am walking alone in the street or in the park as we are walking now, and when evening comes softly and quickly as it has come to-night, the feeling of her comes sharply into my body and mind. After that one meeting I never saw her again. On the next day I was married and I have never gone back into her street. Often however as I am walking along as I am doing now, a quick sharp earthy feeling takes possession of me. It is as though I were a seed in the ground and the warm rains of the spring had come. It is as though I were not a man but a tree.

"And now you see I am married and everything is all right. My marriage is to me a very beautiful fact. If you were to say that my marriage is not a happy one I could call you a liar and be speaking the absolute truth. I have tried to tell you about this other woman. There is a kind of relief in speaking of her. I have never done it before. I wonder why I was so silly as to be afraid that I would give you the impression I am not in love with my wife. If I did not instinctively trust your understanding I would not have spoken. As the matter stands I have a little stirred myself up. To-night I shall think of the other woman. That sometimes occurs. It will happen after I have gone to bed. My wife sleeps in the next room to mine and the door is always left open. There will be a moon to-night, and when there is a moon long streaks of light fall on her bed. I shall awake at midnight to-night. She will be lying asleep with one arm thrown over her head.

"What is it that I am now talking about? A man does not speak of his wife lying in bed. What I am trying to say is that, because of this talk, I shall think of the other woman to-night. My thoughts will not take the form they did during the week before I was married. I will wonder what has become of the woman. For a moment I will again feel myself holding her close. I will think that for an hour I was closer to her than I have ever been to anyone else. Then I will think of the time when I will be as close as that to my wife. She is still, you see, an awakening woman. For a moment I will close my eyes and the quick, shrewd, determined eyes of that other woman will look into mine. My head will swim and then I will quickly open my eyes and see again the dear woman with whom I have undertaken to live out my life. Then I will sleep and when I awake in the morning it will be as it was that evening when I walked out of my dark apartment after having had the most notable experience of my life. What I mean to say, you understand is that, for me, when I awake, the other woman will be utterly gone."

Daughters

There were two Shepard girls, Kate and Wave. Wave was slender. When she walked, she thrust the upper part of her body slightly forward. She had masses of soft hair always slipping from place and falling down. "It won't stay where I put it," said Wave. Her hair was brown, touched with red, and her eyes were brown. Most of the time she wouldn't get up in the morning. She let Kate do all the work about the house, but Kate didn't care if she did.

The Shepards had come to Longville, to live in town. John Shepard got a job working as a section hand on the railroad. He had been a lumberman working in lumber camps ever since he was a boy and didn't like being in town. He came in because of his daughters. Kate, the elder of the girls, wanted to be a schoolteacher. To do that you had to go through high school. Afterwards you had to go through normal school. Kate thought she could do it.

Before moving into Longville, they had lived in a small unpainted frame house in a little valley up in the hills. The house lay six miles back in the hills beyond the Bear Creek settlement and the Bear Creek lumber camp where John Shepard had been working when his wife died. His wife was a huge fat woman with a reputation for laziness. "Look at her house," people said. Her house always was dirty. It was in disorder. It had remained that way until Kate got old enough to take a hand in the housework.

Kate was a girl who could do everything. She had kept the garden behind the house. She milked the cow. She swept and kept the house. She rose before daylight to put the house in order and be in time for school. The girls had had to walk three miles to reach the one-room country schoolhouse. Often they had to wade through snow and, in the spring, through mud. Whenever the weather was bad, when it was cold or rainy, or snow or mud lay deep on the valley road, which followed the windings of a creek, Wave didn't go.

When she did go, she always played in the boys' games. She threw a ball as if she were a boy. She could outrun the boys and sometimes tore into one of them and licked him. She swore like a boy.

"Hell, I'll not go to school, not in this weather. To hell with it," she said. Her mother could not get her to obey.

All through their childhood, the two girls saw little of their father, who often worked in lumber camps. Sometimes, coming home at the weekend after a long hard week of heavy work, and finding his wife sitting in a disordered house, dirty clothes lying about on the floor, and the bed in which he was to sleep with her unmade, and hearing her say she couldn't do anything with Wave, John Shepard, who seldom complained, had spoken almost sharply.

"What's the matter with you, Nan?" he asked. "Can't you run your house? Can't you run your children?"

"I would just like to have you try it, with that Wave," she said. "She's a little hellcat," she added. She said that if you tried to make Wave do something she didn't want to do, she'd just lay on the floor and scream.

"I got a whip and whipped her, but she just kept screaming, screaming and kicking her heels in the air. She wouldn't give in. You couldn't make her give in."

He himself, when at home and in a room with his daughter Wave, always felt a little uncomfortable. He spoke to her and, if she didn't want to, she didn't answer. She could look at you and make you feel uncomfortable. There was something a little queer. Sometimes her eyes seemed to be insulting you. "Don't bother me. Who are you that you should bother me? If I want to answer when you speak to me, I will. If I don't, I won't."

Wave sat in a chair and put her legs up. She put her feet up on the back of another chair. She left her dress all open at the front. She went about barefooted, barelegged. Her legs were dirty. She could sit for a long, long time, saying nothing, staring at you until you wanted to go and cuff her.

And then, suddenly she could grow nice. There was a soft warm look came into her eyes. You wanted to go and take her into your arms, hold her tight, cuddle her, kiss her, but you'd better not try. She might suddenly hit you with her hard, sharp little fists. Once she had done that to her father, and having taken her into his arms he put her quickly down.

"Your mother can't do anything with you, but I'll show that I can," he said. "I was as mad as I ever was in my life," he said afterward, talking with George Russell, a man who worked with him in the woods. "My wife just had two girls," he said. "I wish they had been boys." He explained to the other man how it was about girls. "They are good or they ain't. You can't make them good.

"When they're little things they're nice, but, as soon as they begin to grow up, they bother you. You get to thinking, 'Now what's going to happen to them?'

"There are always boys hanging after young girls," he said. He said that, in the country, girls, when they got to a certain age, were always going into the bushes with boys.

"You can talk to a boy, set him straight, but you can't talk about a thing like that to a girl. How can you?" he asked.

The other man, with whom John Shepard worked, didn't know how you could. He had three sons. He didn't have any girls. "I don't know how you could. I guess you can't," he said.

That time, when Wave hit her father in the face with her fists, because, just then, she didn't want to be held by him, didn't at the moment fancy being caressed by him, John went and cut a switch, a good stout one. He went to where there was a thicket beyond his farm, but, when he came back to his house, Wave wasn't there.

She was sitting astride the roof of his house. He told the man in the woods about it.

"The roof of my house is so steep a cat couldn't climb it, but she climbed it," he said.

She just sat up there, staring down at him.

"Come down," he said.

"Come down," his wife said. His wife was alive then. His wife could sit all day without moving. She took a chair out into the yard and sat in it. "I can sit down here as long as she can sit up there," John's wife said. He thought probably she could. "I never saw a woman could sit as long as my wife can," he said to the man in the woods. He said she could sit anywhere, on a chair, on the ground, even when the ground was wet, on the floor. He said that if his wife, instead of Wave, had been sitting on the roof, he'd have given up at once.

"I gave up, promised I'd never touch her if she came on

down, made my wife promise, because Kate, her sister, cried so hard.

"She just sobbed and sobbed. She was so scared her sister would fall. She's such a good girl that I couldn't say no.

"'Don't touch her, Pa. Please don't touch her. Promise you won't touch her. Make Ma promise,' she kept pleading and she kept sobbing like her heart was breaking, so I promised," he said to the man in the woods. He said he thought that his daughter Wave was just having a good time. "She was enjoying herself, the little hellcat," he said.

It was a year after his wife's death that John Shepard had moved to Longville. He hated it. He didn't want to live in town. He had saved his money and bought a little farm in a nice little valley. Working in the camps he had made plans. A stream ran through the farm, a rapid little stream that came down out of the East Tennessee hills, and he planned to build a dam and run a mill. He would grind corn for people who lived on little farms farther up the valley. A man could get his toll. He could keep enough meal to feed his family and his chickens. He could keep two or three cows, sell the calves, raise hogs. "A man can get along good," he said to another man with whom he worked—always in deep woods. "He can enjoy his family." He was a quiet, slow-speaking man who, even when a young fellow, hadn't gone off, after payday, drinking or whore-hopping like most of the young fellows in the camps.

But he had had a talk with his daughter Kate, one weekend when he was at home, after his wife had died. Kate was nearly fifteen, Wave almost thirteen. It was a Sunday morning and Kate had got his breakfast. She had been up a long time, milked the cow, fed the chickens and

the two pigs. She had brought water from the spring.
John had shaved. He had put on a clean shirt and a clean
pair of overalls. Kate had washed them for him. The little
house was all in order, everything swept, the windows
washed, nothing lying about on the floor in the front
room where the family ate, where they sat. There was a
fireplace and, as the bright spring morning was cold,
Kate had brought in wood and built a fire.

She asked him whether the coffee was good. She got
him a second cup.

Wave was in bed.

"You've been doing all of the work, ain't you?" he
asked, but Kate said no, she hadn't. She brought him
some jelly for his bread and told him Wave had made it.
Wave had baked a cake. Kate began bragging about
Wave. She could make pies. She could bake the lightest
cake you ever ate.

"I can't cook half as good as Wave can," Kate said. She
said Wave could do anything she put her hand to. If she
wanted to and when she went to school, she could be the
smartest one there. Kate got a little excited when she
spoke of her sister. She always did. There was a kind of
shine came into her eyes. It was true, said Kate, that when
there was bad weather or when she didn't want to go, she
wouldn't go to school, but you give her a book, a hard
one, now, any book, and she could read it right off.

She could read a book or a story and then she could tell
about it, make it sound better than when you read it
yourself.

And when she wanted to, she could make clothes. "You
just give her some odd scraps," Kate said. She said that
Wave had taken an old dress that had belonged to their
mother and had cut it up. She had just slashed right into
it. She had made two dresses out of the one dress, one for

herself and one for Kate.

Kate came and sat at the table with her father.

"Pa, we ought to move to town," said she. Her face had
got flushed. It was hard for Kate to talk as she did that
morning. She wanted her father to sell the farm, to try to
get a job in town, and John Shepard thought, listening to
her talk, that Wave had put her up to it.

"I'll bet the little hellcat did put her up to it," he said to
the man who worked with him in the woods. Kate had,
however, said nothing of Wave's wishes. She had been
bragging her sister up and then she stopped. She took it
all on her own shoulders. She said she wanted to 'be a
schoolteacher and had to go to high school. She said that
if they lived in town, in Longville — it was twenty miles
away; it was a big town — if they lived there she bet she
could get a job, maybe in a store. She said she bet she
could do something to help earn money. He told the man
in the woods that, once she had got on the subject, she
didn't let up. She talked that Sunday, and then she talked
every time he went home. He said it wasn't like her. His
daughter, Wave, he knew was back of it, but what could
he do? He said he couldn't say no to Kate, not for long.

"She's such a good girl," he said. He said he couldn't
refuse her anything. "She works so hard. She does everything. She never complains. I guess I got to give her her
chance," he said, and he said he wouldn't mind, he was
getting old, he didn't expect it mattered much where he
worked, although he hated living in town, didn't like it
at all.

He had hoped to spend his old age on his farm. That
was why he had worked and saved to buy it. He expected,
if he sold his farm, he'd only get enough to buy a little
house in town with no ground at all, not to speak of.

"Maybe just enough for a little scrawny garden and it

mighty poor soil," he said. "And I've got my place now pretty well built up. I've been buying fertilizer and putting it on. What my land needs is time," he said.

He said he knew that his youngest daughter was back of Kate's talk about moving to town and being a schoolteacher and all, but that he guessed he couldn't refuse.

It was a little yellow house. You went down a sloping, unpaved street that ended in a swamp, and the yellow house was at the end of the street. It stood on a high gravelly bank above the low swampy land and there were trees, two hickory trees and a beech, their roots reaching down into the black swampland. They stood just where the yard of the yellow house shelved off into the swamp and, just at the base of the beech — a tree with great spreading limbs, one of its great branches lying against the house wall—a spring bubbled up. People came from other houses along the short little street to get water. There had been a barrel sunk into the ground and a stream ran down from the barrel's edge, spreading out over the low black land.

The low land was covered with little grassy hills surrounded by stagnant water. There was a stream that, sometimes in the spring and fall, got out of its banks, covering the low land, but in the summer it was a mere trickle. The stream came out of the town. It went away across fields. You could stand in the yard before the yellow house and look away to long stretches of farm land. There was a big white farmhouse, standing on a low hill in the distance, and back of it was a big red barn.

John Shepard, the lumberman, had sold his little farm in the valley between high hills and bought the yellow house. He hated it, but "What's the use of complaining?" he thought. He had got a job working on the railroad that

went through Longville, was a section hand. He got a
dollar fifty a day. He had bought the house at the town's
edge, because, he thought, "Anyway, it won't be so
crowded."

There wasn't anyone to talk to in town. He was a man
who went cautiously toward others — made friends
slowly. He left the house early in the morning, carried his
lunch pail, and was gone all day. It seemed strange and
unnatural to him not to be in the deep woods, not to have
the smell of the woods in his nostrils. There was that
other man with whom he had worked in the woods, the
fellow that had sons and no daughters. He missed him.
The two men had worked together for a long time. It was
a big cutting they had been on. They had kept going
forward, into hills, swamping-out roads, getting the logs
out. You worked with another man, felling the trees, and
others came and trimmed the logs. You could get ahead
of them, sit down and rest, talk with the other man who
worked with you.

You didn't see much of the boss. You had your life in
there, away deep in there, in the deep woods with the
other man, your pardner.

John Shepard went along through busy town streets,
up and out of the street at the end of which, by the
swampy place, he had his house. He had to go through a
street where there were big houses set in lawns. His
daughter Kate had a job in one of the big houses. She
prepared his breakfast, fixed his lunch pail, and then
went to the big house.

She cooked there. She swept out rooms and made
beds. She wasn't the first girl in the house. She was the
second one. They let her go to school. The woman gave
her dresses. She told her father how nice they were to her.
She said they wanted her to have her chance. "I tell you,

Pa, they're mighty nice to me," she said. She stayed up there at night, after school, working sometimes until eight or even nine o'clock, then she came home and got her father's supper. When there was a party or something up where she worked and she knew she'd be late, she'd slip home after school and get something cold ready for him. Regular evenings, when she had everything cleaned up, she'd sit in the kitchen, at the kitchen table, studying.

Wave wasn't there. She was off somewhere, traipsing around with the town boys. She never seemed to want to eat much. She didn't mind missing a meal. Sometimes quite late at night, when Kate had got through studying and had gone to bed and when John Shepard was in bed, a car drove up before the house and Wave got out.

He could hear some man's voice. He could hear the car turn.

Most of the dresses Kate had given her, working up there in the rich people's house, Wave got.

She could take a dress and change it. She could make it something new. If it was out of style, she could put it back in style. She could take two dresses and make one. Wave wasn't afraid of anyone or anything. Kate, when she had time to talk to her father, maybe in the evening after the evening meal, when she was washing dishes and cleaning up and he was on the steps by the kitchen door smoking his pipe before going to bed, continued bragging Wave up.

"I wish I could cook like Wave can.

"She can do anything she sets her hand to.

"If I could fix up dresses as well as she can, I'll bet I'd have a shop."

John said nothing. It made him sore to hear Kate talk so.

"If she can cook so good, why don't she stay home and get my supper?" he thought. Sometimes he thought, "Kate is away all day and so am I. She's just bound to get

herself into trouble and bring disgrace on us." Sometimes
he wanted to spank Wave. He came home from work and
there she was, on the front porch, sitting in a chair, her
legs up on another chair. She didn't seem to mind what
she showed. She'd show everything she had. She was
always reading. She got books somewhere, Kate said
from a free library. She didn't care if there was someone
coming along the street. The people on that street were
always coming down to the spring, under the trees, at
the edge of the bank, right near the front of the house.
There were women coming. Men came. There were
some of the men who were young fellows. They worked
in a factory in town.

Wave didn't care. She'd dress up, like a doll, right in the
morning, when she first got up. Sometimes she didn't get
up until noon. She turned night into day. She was there,
like that, on the porch, reading a book, maybe just waiting for some man to come in a car and take her out, God
only knew to where, when John Shepard came home.

He asked her if she had got his supper and she didn't
answer. She didn't even look at him and he wanted to
snatch the book out of her hands. He wanted to take her
across his knees. She wasn't very big. She was slender and
not very strong. He wanted to take her on his knees and
spank her behind.

"I'd like to fan her little behind for her," he thought.

Sometimes when John Shepard came home from his
work and Wave was there sitting maybe on the porch, not
answering when he spoke to her, her feet up on another
chair or on the porch rail, reading a book, and when Kate
hadn't got a chance to slip home and get something ready
for him and he got mad, he thought, "Kate wouldn't like
it. She wouldn't stand for it," he thought. When that
happened, sometimes he got a headache.

It was because he was so mad and could do nothing. It was because it was Wave who was behind Kate's wanting to come live in town. It was because Wave kept putting all the work on Kate.

"I don't know how she got to be like she is," he told himself. He hated to think about her. He didn't want to. When he thought about fanning her little behind, he got excited. It was an odd excitement. It made his head ache. It made his back ache. When he was in the woods cutting down trees, he always did heavy work, but he never had a backache or headache, but when he got mad at Wave and could do nothing because there was nothing he could do, he did.

It wasn't the work he was doing, on the railroad. He knew that. It wasn't such heavy work.

He hated being alone in the house with Wave. She could make him furious just looking at him. Sometimes, when he came home from work, and she was there and Kate wasn't — he couldn't stay. He kept opening and closing his fists. Even if it was winter and if Wave was at home and not traipsing around with some man and there was snow on the ground, he went out of the house.

He went into the back yard. There wasn't much front yard, but the back yard was long. When he had bought the place, he had thought that maybe he would raise chickens. He never had. "I don't seem to get around to begin," he said to himself. He thought maybe it was Wave's fault.

He stood about. He was waiting for Wave to go away or Kate to come home. When it was dark, he sat sometimes on the ground, under one of the hickory trees. The hickory trees were at the back of the yard where the ground shelved off, down to the swamp. The beech tree was in front, right by the street. He got so mad that he beat the ground with his open hand. One night he beat so hard that the gravelly soil hurt his hand. He didn't mind the hurt. He liked it, but afterwards his back ached and his head ached. It spoiled his supper.

A porch extended along one side of the little yellow house and faced the street. Through a door in the side porch you entered a small parlor, behind which lay a bedroom, where the girls slept. The kitchen was built on. The stairs to the upper story mounted out of the girls' room. There was no door at its head, and the stairs came right into the room where John Shepard had his bed. A wooden railing had been placed beside the stair pit, there, so that in case you did not light a lamp when you went to bed, or got up in the night or early in winter, you wouldn't in the darkness fall through the opening. There was a second room in the upper story, and to reach it you had to pass through John Shepard's

He was wandering restlessly about in the back yard. It was evening. A car drove up and Wave got into it. She was "stepping out." "I'm stepping out, Kid," she would have said to her sister, fixing herself up. Wave, although younger than Kate, always called her sister "Kid." It was the assertion of a kind of superiority perhaps in worldly knowledge, which Kate didn't mind. Kate never minded anything Wave said or did. John Shepard heard a man's voice out in the road. The fellow had to turn the car and John got behind one of the hickories. He didn't want the car's headlight to search him out, find him wandering there. Anyway, he didn't want Wave to know she could worry him.

He went into the house. Kate was sitting in the kitchen by the table. She was sitting under a kerosene lamp, as the Shepards didn't have electric lights. She had a book open.

It was nice and clean in there. When Kate was in the house even for just a little while, she got everything looking and smelling nice. He thought Kate was very pretty. He thought she was beautiful. Sometimes when he admired her he wondered how she had come to be as fine as she was, and was disloyal to his dead wife. "She isn't much like her Ma or me either," thought he.

"Where you been, Pa?" Kate asked, and he said he had just stepped outside. He wanted to tell her that he couldn't bear being in the house when Wave was there. He wasn't a swearing man, but he wanted to say "Goddam Wave. I wish she'd get the hell out of my house and stay out." He wanted to say, "I don't give a goddam what happens to her. I can't bear being in the goddam house when she's here. "

Sometimes he said such things aloud, when he was going to work, in the early morning, hardly anyone in the streets, even in Main Street, through which he had to pass, just maybe a few clerks, opening up and sweeping out stores. He said such things aloud, then or in the evening when he was coming home. But he knew he couldn't say them to Kate.

He said, "I guess I'll go on to bed." He didn't want to go to bed, but he didn't want to interrupt her in her studies. He thought, "Maybe I could just sit down here, near her, and smoke my pipe.

"I like to be near her," he thought.

He thought, "I never liked to be near her Ma, even when she was a young girl, before she got so fat, when I was courting her, like I like to be near Kate.

"But maybe it would bother her, me sitting about," he thought.

"And anyway," he thought, "I don't enjoy smoking when I've got a headache."

He hesitated, standing back of Kate, who was absorbed in her book.

She turned and saw him.

She had got a new lamp shade on her lamp. "Look at it, Pa," she said. "Ain't it pretty?" She said that Wave had made it. His headache got worse.

"Goddam Wave," he thought.

"She's sure got fine eyes," he thought, looking at her. He was always wondering, since he came to live in town, why it was that men and boys all seemed to be crazy to be with Wave and why so few got after Kate. He thought it showed that town men hadn't a bit of sense.

"If I was a young fellow now," he thought, "and Kate wasn't my daughter—"

He had gone to stand near the door that led into Kate's and Wave's room and to the foot of the stairs.

"I'd better not sit down," he thought. If he sat down he'd be staying. She worked hard. "She ought to get her studying done and go to bed," he thought.

Kate had been talking about the room upstairs, the one at the front of the house. She had said that sometimes she thought she'd better put an ad in the paper. "We could get something for the room and it would be a help." If, as sometimes happened, she also spoke of wanting to buy something for Wave, speaking maybe of Wave's birthday coming, or maybe Christmas, mentioning maybe a pair of silk stockings, something like that, it spoiled things. But sometimes she didn't mention Wave at all, and when she talked in her intimate way, Wave gone, it seemed to him that his back and head both were feeling better.

Kate began speaking about the roomer for the room above, giving the impression that she had given the matter a lot of thought.

"If it was a young fellow now, a quiet one."

She was attending the town high school. There were young fellows, also from the country, who came to town to school, some drove into town in cars, but others had no cars.

"If we had a young fellow like that, in the other room, upstairs, he and I could talk over our lessons."

Kate said that some of the lessons she had to take in school were mighty hard for her. She had to study a thing called Latin.

"What's that?" her father asked, and she said it was a language.

"It's the way people talked, a long time ago," she explained. She said they wrote books in a language different from the one she and her father talked. She didn't know why you had to learn to read books written in it, but you did. If she was ever going to get a chance as a schoolteacher, she had to learn it.

"Even if we got only a dollar a week," she continued. "It couldn't be a girl, up there with you, having to go back and forth through your room. If he wanted his breakfast, I could get it while I am getting yours."

She continued earnestly talking of the possible roomer. Suddenly it occurred to her father that she was describing a real person. She spoke so definitely of him.

John Shepard went upstairs and to bed. For some time a vague resentment against young men had been growing in him. Going to work and coming from it he had begun looking closely at young men he met. Now and then one of them, who came in the evening for Wave—he might be going to take her for a ride in his car — there seemed an endless stream of the men, some younger than others, big ones and little ones, men well dressed, others rather shabbily dressed — now and then one of them sat for a time on the side porch of the house.

He would himself have fled into the back yard. Wrath was rising in him. "What's she up to?" It must be, he thought, that half the town was talking about his daughter.

"I don't believe all of these men would be after her unless —"

There were thoughts he couldn't finish, didn't want to finish.

If she were going all the way with them, one after another —

Wrath boiled up in him.

But, lying in bed, it seemed to him that the young roomer was in the house. He was in the room at the front of the house, just beyond his own, behind the closed door. He was in there studying as Kate was studying below in the kitchen. . . . Now he was below with her, talking their lessons over with her. . . . He was quietly coming upstairs.

John Shepard had always wanted a son. The young man would be like Kate, not like Wave, a fellow always running around in the streets at night, crazy after girls as Wave was crazy after boys.

The resentment returned. The young fellow who had come for Wave earlier in the evening had returned with her, was sitting down on the porch with her. The two were laughing and talking together.

"Now quit that, smarty," he heard Wave say to the man.

He would have been grabbing her leg or something like that. It sounded like it.

She wasn't mad, though. She laughed when she told the fellow to quit it. She didn't sound as though she meant it. She had a curiously soft silvery laugh. She began singing.

She could do all sorts of things Kate couldn't do and that was annoying too.

For example she could sing. She had a curiously soft,

clear, penetrating voice. Late at night, when she had come home, after an evening spent with some man and had got into bed with Kate and was telling Kate of her adventures and was speaking in a low voice, hardly more than a whisper, her father, in his bed upstairs could hear every word she said.

Kate had a rather husky voice. It sounded as though she were catching cold. Her father was always asking, "You ain't catching cold, are you, Kate?"

"Why, no," she said.

Wave knew a lot of songs. She'd sing songs to the men that weren't very nice. She sang a song about a girl who got pregnant by some man she wasn't married to. It was called "Careless Love." It was about a girl who got big with child so that she couldn't tie her apron strings. The strings wouldn't go around her swollen belly. The man who did it to her, after he had done it, wouldn't marry her.

It wasn't any song to sing, to just any man, especially when you weren't married to him. Wave sang it in her soft, low, clear voice, and John Shepard was sure she could be heard all along the street at the end of which they lived.

God only knew what people thought.

But, just the same, in spite of yourself, when Wave sang like that...you just couldn't help yourself...you began to like her in spite of yourself.

The singing seemed to carry John Shepard back into his young manhood. He was again a young lumberman. On Saturday night he was in a town near the lumber camp where he worked then. He had gone into town with other young lumbermen.

They were drinking and fighting. They were going whore-hopping, out to raise hell, but he wasn't. He walked about. The town was small, but he got off the main street.

There was a house, halfway up a hill, a half mile out of town. It had apple trees in the yard.

There was an old man with a gray beard, who walked with a stick. There was an old blind woman.

There was a young girl, very slender, very pretty. They had mosquito netting about the porch of their house.

On warm clear nights they brought a lamp out there and the young girl read aloud to the old white-bearded man and to the blind woman.

Her voice was like a bird singing away off somewhere in the deep woods.

The first time when John Shepard, as a young man, had gone into the town and when wandering about, not wanting to drink and raise hell with the others, not wanting to go whore-hopping — he didn't believe in it; it was against his principles — he had often said to himself, "I'll wait 'til I get honestly married ... "

"I'm not just an animal ... " he had said.

"I'll go clean to her. I'll be asking her to come clean to me and I ought to go clean to her. ... "

There was deep dust in the road and when he went past that house, that was quite near the road. They didn't see him. They didn't hear him. There was a kind of hedge and he sat down under it. He hadn't ever thought that he could get a woman like the one on the porch of that house, reading aloud to the two old people, so beautiful, so evidently refined.

He thought, "I'll bet she's educated. She reads so well." He thought maybe she had just come there, to that town, maybe to visit her grandmother and grandfather.

"I'll bet, at home, she's away up in life," he thought. He imagined all sorts of things about her, creeping back to hide under the hedge, on many Saturday nights, always dreaming and thinking about her all week when he was at work in the woods. Bitterly disappointed when, having gone into town and up there, she wasn't on the porch reading to the old people, so disappointed that sometimes he cried.

Not that he had ever thought he could get such a woman.

He had never even spoken to her. How could he have gotten a chance, he told himself, and if a chance had come, what could he have said? She had been there with the two old people and then she wasn't there. He guessed she was just visiting there, in that house, in that town. He guessed they were her grandparents. It had been like spring coming after a long hard winter in the woods. Spring comes, and then after a while, it isn't spring any more.

What annoyed John Shepard, though, was that Wave, sitting singing on the porch to a man she had picked up, should rouse a funny feeling in her father. Making him think of his youth when he went creeping up a hillside road, out of a lumber town, hiding under bushes, seeing another young woman on the porch of a house, himself full of a mysterious love that made him sit by the roadside silently crying, just as if, he told himself, a man, certainly a very ordinary man, not educated, one who always had lived with rough uncouth men, drinkers, fighters and whore-hoppers, had fallen in love with an angel sitting on a star up in the sky. As if she herself, the little devil down there, were an angel sitting on a star. The singing carried you up to her. It seemed to float you. Made you as if in a dream where your feet leave the earth and you float like a bird up in the sky.

It made him angry. God knows he had seen and heard enough of his daughter Wave. In spite of himself, though, he quit wanting to fan her little behind, and went to sleep.

He awoke. Kate was up, getting his breakfast. It was lucky that, at the place where she worked, they didn't have their breakfast early like that. John guessed they stayed in bed. "How they can, when it's broad daylight, say now in the summer, I don't know," he thought.

"I like the early part of the day," he thought. He remembered how, when he was still working in the woods, he went from where he slept, in a bunk in a little shack, usually with two or three others to where they all ate their breakfast.

It would be hardly day. It would be a pinkness. You went along a creek and crossed on a log. There was good woods smells and good food smells. In a lumber camp, no one talked while they were eating. It was a rule they had. It wasn't a law. It was a rule. It was in all lumber camps. It made it nice.

You ate and got on a car, a flat one, part of a lumber train, and you went along a creek.

There were some began to talk, but John didn't. He sat silent, at the edge of a flatcar, his legs hanging down.

There was a kingfisher bird, up early and on a limb, a dead limb hanging out over the stream. There was a quiet above the talk of the men. There was a squirrel went up the trunk of a tree.

It was all nice. It was funny to think there were people in towns who wanted to stay in bed.

"I couldn't. Even if I had a million dollars, I couldn't," thought John Shepard.

He went downstairs and there was Wave in bed asleep. She had kicked the covers off again. You could see clear up her leg, all of it, and see her little behind.

He was in bed again. He had been talking with Kate again about the roomer for the room next his.

"It gets kind of real," he thought.

"I guess now he'd be down there with Kate," he thought. Sometimes, when he was in bed like that, not asleep yet, not wanting to go to sleep, not feeling like sleep, he could almost see the young man.

"He'd have to be a pretty sensible one." He thought it would be nice if the young man was good-looking, but not too good-looking. He might be smart and quick at things, like Wave was—at least like Kate was always saying Wave was — but, he thought, not too goddam smart. "Smart enough, though, not to fall for Wave," he thought.

He thought, "He'd be down there with Kate, she helping him, he helping her, but she wouldn't be showing her legs. Nothing like that," he thought.

He thought... "Maybe they'd both be like I was about that one on the porch that time. Like that about each other," he thought.

It got so that, having these thoughts, night after night, they got more and more real.

Sometimes he thought, when he went upstairs to bed, when he was undressing, he thought ... "No, he ain't down there with Kate.

"He's in there. He's in his room.

"He's studying now. I got to be mighty careful.

"I can't make any noise," he thought.

He argued with himself. "The fellow can't be down there with Kate, sitting with her, studying with her, liking her, gradually getting more and more stuck on her, because I just came up from there.

"He's in there in his room, studying now," he thought.

"If he comes through the room here, going down to be with Kate, I'll pretend to be asleep." He thought of something that gave him a lot of satisfaction. "There's a lot of men that snore when they sleep, but I don't," he thought. There had been a fellow at the lumber camp where he worked. He came to bunk in the same shack. He said, "Thank God, you don't snore." He said it in the morning after the first night in the shack with John. He said, "Christ, the bedbugs are as bad here as where I was where I worked last, but thank God, you ain't no snorer." He said that, in the last camp where he had worked, he had been put in to bunk in a shack with a man who snored so that he raised the goddam roof. He said the fellow made the goddam roof flop up and down like a goddam tent that hadn't, he said, been pegged down.

"You know, he said, "like a goddam tent in a goddam storm." He meant to say that John didn't snore when he slept.

"And I'm glad I don't," John thought. He thought he'd hate to be bothering the roomer he and Kate were always speaking about. "Either," he thought, "when he's up here in his room or when he's down there sitting with Kate."

Lying there, arguing with himself in bed, upstairs in his house, John Shepard heard the sound of voices. His daughter Wave had been out with one of her men. She had come home and she and Kate were in bed.

They were talking. They were laughing. There was a fat girl who worked in the house where Kate worked.

She couldn't get any men. Kate was telling Wave a story. The fat girl, who worked at that place where Kate worked, wrote letters to herself. Kate said she had seen one of the letters.

The fat girl had let it fall on the floor. It fell out of the pocket of her apron. Her name was Evelyn. "Darling Evelyn," the letter began. The fat girl couldn't spell very well. Kate said the fat girl went down into the town. She went to a florist. She bought a box of roses and sent them to herself. She had, Kate said to Wave, gone somewhere and had some cards printed. There was a man's name on the cards.

She put one of the cards into the box of roses. She had it addressed to herself. She had it sent to the house where she worked. She left the box open. Kate saw the card lying in the box on the roses.

"When she was down in the kitchen, I went into her room. She had got a whole pack of the cards printed. They were in a little pasteboard box in there. The name printed on the cards was 'Robert Huntington.'"

There wasn't any such man. Kate and Wave were lying downstairs. They were laughing at the fat girl. Wave was telling Kate about some man.

"He wanted to kiss me.

"He put his hand on my leg."

They began talking in lowered voices. Wave was telling Kate what some man had tried to do to her. Occasionally the two girls giggled, and John Shepard silently got out of bed.

He was barefooted. He slept in the same shirt he wore during the day. At night, when he went to bed he just took off his shoes, his socks and his pants. He shivered as he went silently down the stairs. He stood there near the foot of the stairs.

Wave was telling Kate how far she thought it was safe to let the men go. She was saying that there was one man who had almost got her.

"I let him go a little too far."

"What did you let him do?"

Wave had begun to whisper. It was almost as though she knew someone was listening. Kate was living her life in Wave's life. As Wave whispered, she giggled.

Kate also giggled.

It was all strange. It was in some way terrible to hear. Kate was feeling what Wave had felt. When she giggled, it was not as it was when Wave giggled. There was something in the tone of the low laughter that came from Kate that made her father shiver again.

He got suddenly angry. He wanted to run and choke Wave. He wanted to drag her out of the bed. He wanted to fan her behind, fan it hard.

He went silently back up the stairs and got into the bed.

There was the fat girl who wrote letters to herself. She sent herself flowers. Kate was living her life in Wave's life. Something not nice, he felt, was going on his house. It seemed to him that Wave, coming into the silent house at night and talking with Kate, had brought something in that spoiled things.

The conversation between his daughters went on. John Shepard was very angry. He was so angry that little beads of sweat stood out on his forehead. He was as he sometimes was in the darkness in the back yard. In the back yard he pounded the ground with his hand. Now he pounded the bedclothes. His head ached and his back hurt.

John Shepard and his daughter Kate got their young man. Kate had put an ad in the paper The young man had taken the room upstairs in the Shepard house. He was in the house. He was in and out. His feet were on the stairs. He was doing exactly as John Shepard had dreamed he would do.

He was a student in the town high school and, apparently, a very studious, earnest young man. He had his breakfast in the house. Like Kate and John Shepard himself, he got up early in the morning. His name was Ben Hurd and, like John himself, he had come to town from a lumber camp. He was a tall, slender young fellow. He had black hair and dark eyes.

He had got a job in town. He was at a store. He went there in the early morning, opened the store and swept out. Then he hurried off to school and after school, in the late afternoon, he returned to the store.

He stayed at the store until ten o'clock at night and then he came to the Shepard house.

John Shepard waited for his coming. Kate waited. John wondered if he was going to study with her. John would be upstairs in his room. He would be in bed with his light out.

John had become neat. When he went to bed at night, he had always just let his clothes lie on the floor, but now he folded his pants. There was a small chest of drawers and he put socks in a drawer and his shoes under the bed. "There isn't any light, but a man might as well learn to be neat," he thought. Kate had got him some pajamas to wear. She said, "Pa, you'd better put these on at night." She said that men in town wore them. He said he'd never heard of any such thing.

"It's what the man does where I work," she said.

"All right," he said.

And Kate had got so she wished she didn't have to work as a servant. She told her father about that. "It isn't such hard work, but it's being a servant. They look down on you," she said.

She said she wished she could get some other work. "Of course," she said, "if I was working, say now in a store, I wouldn't be having clothes and things given to me." She said she was glad Wave didn't have to be a servant. She said she was determined Wave shouldn't be one. When she got to be a schoolteacher, she was going to save her money. She had a plan. She and Wave would have a shop. She thought sometimes it would be a millinery shop and at other times she thought it would be a dressmaking shop.

She thought it would be better even than being a schoolteacher. She and Wave could be together. "You wouldn't have to work so hard, Pa," she said.

John Shepard said nothing. When she talked like that, dragging Wave in, he kept still. "To hell with Wave," he thought, but he didn't say it.

He had to stand and listen to Kate talk. It was Wave this and Wave that. Kate was worried because she thought that, because she had to work as a servant, people would look down on them.

When Wave didn't do a damn thing, just loafed about the house, didn't go to school to improve herself, spent all her time fussing with her clothes and her hair, Kate didn't complain.

"Ain't she got nice hair! Ain't it soft! Ain't it pretty!" Kate said.

When she went on about Wave sometimes John Shepard could hardly stand it. He had to clinch his fist. He had to stand and listen. When, in the evening, after the young fellow came to room in the house and Wave wasn't at home—she had a date, she wasn't there—and John was standing by the door, talking to Kate, who was by the kitchen table, sitting there, her schoolbooks on the table, her lamp on the table, and John was having a little talk with Kate and it got on Wave, he just waited, saying nothing until she got through. Then he said, "Good night.

"I guess you want to study. I guess I'll say good night," he said.

He went upstairs. He got into bed. He didn't sleep.

He wondered if Ben Hurd, when he came, would stop and talk maybe with Kate. He thought, "I'll bet Wave don't get him.

"I'll bet he's got more sense than to fool with her," he thought.

"He looks to me like a sensible young fellow," he thought.

"They'd make a nice couple," he thought. Sometimes when Ben Hurd came after ten, and Wave wasn't at home and Kate was down there waiting up—no matter how late it was she always stayed up until Wave came—she and Ben Hurd would talk a little.

They didn't much at first because the young fellow was shy and Kate was shy but then they did, more and more.

A little more and a little more. Not studying together as John Shepard had thought maybe they would, but just talking.

Like, "How do you like it here in town?" or, "How do you like it working in a store?"

It was a dry-goods store. It was a kind of general store. It was owned by a Jew. He didn't have just the one store. He had different stores in different towns.

He came and he went away. Ben Hurd told Kate about the store. He stood by the door downstairs, just as John did himself when he talked to Kate.

"Won't you sit down?" Kate said. She offered him things.

"Won't you have a cup of coffee? I'll make you some.

"Won't you have a glass of milk?"

She offered him a piece of pie. "I'll bet you're hungry." She bragged about the pie. She said Wave made it. She'd begin telling him about Wave, what good pies she could make, what good cake, what good fudge.

There'd be some of her fudge, in a dish on the table downstairs. "Won't you have some?" Kate would say to young Ben Hurd. "I don't care if I do," he'd say. He'd go over to where she was and get a piece, but he wouldn't sit down.

"I got to get upstairs," the young fellow would say to Kate and, instead of sitting awhile, down there with her, he'd come on up. He'd go through John Shepard's room and into his own room.

He'd light his lamp in there. He'd study awhile and then he'd write.

"What the hell's he writing?" John Shepard wondered. The young fellow, Ben Hurd, would write and write. He'd be leaning over his desk. Maybe Wave would come home and she and Kate would go to bed. They'd laugh and talk. Wave would be telling Kate about some man. "He got pretty gay," she'd say. She'd swear sometimes.

Sometimes the young fellow, in the room up there, had left his door a little open. Wave called some man she had been out with a son-of-a-bitch.

"The son-of-a-bitch thought he could get me." She laughed when she said it. It made John Shepard furious. "I'll bet he can hear," thought he. It made him mad that, when Wave spoke in this way, Kate didn't mind. "He'll think Kate's like Wave is," thought he.

He was glad the young fellow had a job, had to work. If he was around the house when Wave was at home, very likely she'd get him. She'd rope him in. She'd do it just to show she could. Once twice, after the young man came to room in the house and when he had come upstairs and was in his room — but not in bed — sitting in there and writing like he did — the door into John's room maybe a

little open—no door downstairs, at the foot of the stairs—
Wave coming home, talking down there — Sometimes
she'd ask—

"What's this young fellow like?" she asked.

"Is he a live wire or is he dead on his feet?" she asked.

She'd say he looked to her like a goody-goody.

"Why don't you find out about him?" she'd ask Kate.

She'd go on like that, maybe saying that if Kate didn't
want him maybe she'd take a whirl at him herself.

"Hush. Be careful. He's up there. He'll hear," Kate
would say, but Wave didn't seem to care. She'd go right on.

"He's yours. You saw him first. I don't want to cut in on
you," Wave would say, and then she'd laugh and Kate
would laugh, and if the door to the young man's room
was even a little open and a streak of light from his lamp
falling into John's room, John Shepard would silently get
out of bed and shut the door.

He went up into the main street of the town. It was
after dark and Wave was at home. He had run out of
tobacco for his pipe and wasn't in a very good mood. He
had been sitting at the supper table alone. Kate had got
his supper and had put it on the back of the stove. She
had set the table. He had to get his own supper off the
stove and put it on the table.

It had made him sore because Wave was right there.
She was in the girls' bedroom.

"I suppose she's dolling up," he had thought. There
would be some man coming for her. "It gets so that my
food doesn't do me any good. I get so I can't digest it," he
thought.

He hadn't anyone to say such things to. "If a man can
talk things over with another man he don't mind so
much," he thought. He had thought that a lot of times

since he had been living in town. ...

He had been remembering when he used to work in the woods, most of the time with just that one other man, George Russell.

A man likes to talk about his work. On the section, where John worked after he came to town, there were two Italians. There was a Negro. There was a German.

The foreman was a silent man. On lots of days, except to tell the men what to do, he never said a word. He was a man who didn't believe in getting too friendly with men working for him. You were out in the open. You were on the railroad. You didn't hear nice sounds, far off, like in the woods.

In the woods it was almost like in church. There was a something solemn. There was a close feeling you had with your pardner. When you got ahead of the knot bumpers, you could sit down, have a pipe with him. You spoke about other times, when you were a young fellow, what you did, things you felt.

You talked about your wives and your families. You told about how it was in another camp where you had worked, before you worked with George. ...

On the main street he went into the drugstore that kept his brand of tobacco. Some young town boys and girls were sitting in the store, in some little booths, open at the side. There was a girl with her legs crossed, her dress, he thought, pulled pretty far up. There was a man sitting with her and they were having some kind of a drink.

The girl had made him think again of Wave. She probably came into that place with men, sat in there showing herself off as she did sitting on the porch at home. He went out of the drugstore—and ran into George Russell coming along the street.

There was a gladness. There was a jumping of the heart.

"Why, hello!"

"Well, I'm damned. It's you. Hello, John."

They went walking along together. George Russell was in town to see his oldest boy off on a train.

"He just left, ten minutes ago."

He was proud. Right away he began telling John about his son.

"Yep," he said, "he's going to go to college. He's been a good boy. He's saved up his money."

He was boy crazy about books. He was smart. He hadn't enough money to pay his way through college, but he was going to start.

He figured maybe he could work on his way through, when he got a start.

He wanted to be a lawyer.

"I'll bet he makes it too. I'll just bet he does," George said.

The two men walked along.

"How do you like it in town, John?"

"I don't like it. I did it on account of my girls. Where you staying, George?"

George was staying in a little hotel on a side street and the two went there.

John was ashamed. "Hell, I'd like to have you at the house, but we ain't got no bed."

George said he had intended looking John up. "I didn't rightly know where you live. I was going to ask," he said.

John thought, "Ain't it hell I can't ask him to come? I ought to ask him to come stay at my house. But hell, who'd cook for him?" he thought. "Not Wave. She'd let him starve," he thought. "Or sit him down maybe to a cold picked-up supper while she went hell-catting around, riding with men in automobiles, sitting in drugstores with men."

The two sat in some chairs on the porch before the hotel where George was staying, right across from the station of the railroad on which John worked. George said he knew the young fellow who was rooming in John's house. He was a good boy. He was all right. He thought maybe John knew his mother, but John said he didn't. He hadn't lived near the mill, he had lived on his farm. "That's right," George said. He talked about his boys. Two of them were all right and good steady boys, but the youngest one he thought wasn't much good. He said the boy was lazy. "And he's a damn little liar." He couldn't account for the boy. He wasn't like George himself and he wasn't like his mother.

The two men talked until quite late, and when George had got through bragging about his son who had gone away to college, John Shepard bragged up his Kate. He wasn't going to say anything about Wave, but then suddenly he did. He told everything, how she was everlasting chasing around with men, how she wouldn't do any work about the house, how she put it all on Kate.

"I'd like to fan her behind. I would, too, if it wasn't for Kate. I don't understand why Kate's like she is about Wave. She takes everything from her. I don't understand it," he said.

He was thinking how much better it must be to have boys than just girls. "You just can't understand a girl," he thought. But he thought, anyway, that George had one boy who wasn't much good. But George was talking about the woods. He was going back to his job in the early morning. There had been a big boundary he and George had worked on together, but now, George said, it was almost cleaned up. George had said he reckoned, pretty soon, he'd be in another camp. "There isn't much big timber left," George had said. "Pretty soon," George said, "there'd only be little pickerwood mills." George had said he wasn't worried. He reckoned his oldest son would get to be a lawyer. He was a good boy. He'd take care of George.

"I don't mean I'd want to go and live with him, not after he gets married." What George meant was that his son, when he had got to be a lawyer, would maybe, every month, send his father some money.

John didn't start home till nearly eleven. He was a little excited, felt it had done him good to have the talk with his friend. He didn't go right home. Ever since he had come to live in town he had been pretty lonely, but now he felt as he used to feel, when as a young fellow he went off to town with other young lumbermen on a Saturday night. He walked around. He was in quiet residential streets. He was down by the railroad. He was by a dark warehouse. There was a man in there, in his shirt sleeves, under a light, leaning over a desk. He seemed to be writing. Lots of nights Ben Hurd in his room in the Shepard house also wrote that way under the lighted lamp. Some people worked like that over books, in a warehouse, one studying to be a schoolteacher, another to be a lawyer like George Russell's boy. Some of them got rich. They lived in big houses. He thought maybe Ben Hurd and his Kate would get married and be like that.

"I wouldn't want to be like that myself," he thought. "I'd rather be a workingman in a lumber camp, or anyway just go on until I get too old, just working."

"But a man does get old," he thought that night as he walked through streets and past houses. Once he found himself again in front of the little hotel where he had sat and talked with George Russell.

"He don't want to live with them when he's old," he thought, his mind running on George Russell's boy, grown to be a lawyer and married, George grown old, not able to work any longer, and then on young Ben Hurd, married to his Kate, gotten to be a businessman, maybe, owning a warehouse, or a store, or maybe being a lawyer, like George's boy.

He supposed maybe his Wave might get married too. "If she does, I pity the man. I pity him," he thought.

He decided he'd better be home. He went through dark streets. "It must be past midnight," he thought.

He went along his own street. There was a light in his house, in the kitchen of his house.

He got off the sidewalk. He got into the road. He didn't know afterward why he did it.

He could see there was a light in the kitchen of his house. He went past in the dusty road. The street ended in the black swamp, but it was summer and the swamp was almost dried up. He went through it. He got into his own gravelly back yard.

He could hear voices.

"It's Wave," he thought.

He thought, "She's sitting on the porch. She's got a man out there. Goddam her," he thought.

He went silently up to the kitchen window and looked in. Kate was sitting in there. She had her book open, but she wasn't studying.

She was crying. She was crying silently, as he once had done, lying under a hedge by a road, near a house where there was a young girl sitting with two old people on a porch.

There was a man's voice on the porch. Wave was out there. John went into the shed that was back of his house. When he was in the shed he could see through a crack.

There was light come out from Kate's lamp onto the porch. Young Ben Hurd was there. He was sitting there with Wave. They were sitting close. He had his arm around Wave.

He must have done something with his hand.

"Now you quit," she said.

She called him a "smarty."

"You quit it, smarty," she said, and then she laughed.

She moved a little away from him. She put her legs up. The way she was sitting, the light coming out from the kitchen, through an open door, and the way young Ben Hurd was sitting, he could see plenty, all right.

"Goddam! She's showing him all she's got," her father thought.

He felt frozen. He felt cold. He just stood.

And then she began to sing. Her voice was like that of the girl on the porch of another house when he was young. There was the same clearness, the same strange sweetness.

There was tenderness. There was something like a bird singing.

It was something he couldn't stand, that had always made him furious.

She sang, and then she stopped. Ben Hurd tried to kiss her, but she wouldn't let him. She stood by a post. Her soft mass of hair had slipped down. They talked in low tones. "Good night," she said. She made him go away. She kept saying, "Good night."

She pushed him away, made him go away.

He went upstairs. John Shepard heard him go up the stairs.

Wave just sat on the porch. She put her legs up again. She sang again and John Shepard rushed out of the shed.

He ran to where she was. He got his hand on her throat. He choked her.

She struggled, but he had her down on the floor of the

porch. She scratched his face. She kicked him, but he fanned her behind.

He fanned her behind with his open hand. He had her dress up. His palm struck her flesh. He fanned it hard. He kept fanning it. His hand pressed hard on her throat. He had her, she could not make a sound.

"By God, I'd 'a' killed her, I guess I'd 'a' choked her to death, if it hadn't been for Kate."

Kate had come running out. She had begun hitting him with her fist. She kept pleading. She didn't plead loud. She didn't want Ben Hurd to hear.

Ben was upstairs. He remained silent.

Kate's voice was far off. It was like in a dream. It was far off and then it got a little nearer.

It came in to him. His mind was a house and the door of the house was closed. It came open. Kate's voice pleading and pleading made it come open. He let go of Wave's throat. He quit fanning her flesh. She was very white, lying on the porch, in the light from Kate's lamp.

"Maybe she's dead," he thought, and he went away. He went into the gravelly back yard. He sat down out there. His head ached and his back hurt.

He could see through a window into the kitchen. He didn't know how long it was, but he saw Kate in there.

He saw Wave. She wasn't dead.

"I didn't kill her, goddam it. I didn't kill her," he thought. He sat a long time, his head aching and his back hurting.

"I guess they're going to bed," he thought.

"I 'll bet they ain't laughing or talking now," he thought.

He sat and sat and then he went to bed himself. He went upstairs through their room.

"I got to be quiet," he thought. That young Ben Hurd was in his room. "I'm glad I don't snore when I sleep," he thought. Ben Hurd's door was a little open and he went softly and silently and closed it. He got into bed. He saw the sky through a window in his room. He saw the stars. He wanted to cry, but he didn't. He just stayed still, looking at the stars and wishing his head would quit aching and his back quit hurting, until presently he heard his two daughters in their room downstairs.

They were laughing and talking. They talked in low tones and then they laughed. There was something incomprehensible. His head didn't quit aching and his back didn't quit hurting. They ached and they hurt worse than ever. He thought he wouldn't get any sleep.

"I'll bet I don't," he thought. "I'll be tired tomorrow." He thought of the men in the woods. He wished he was like George Russell, who'd had boys. Girls were something you couldn't understand.

The sound of the whispering continued. Girls were something you couldn't understand. There was something—it was hidden from you. How strange it was!

Milk Bottles

I lived, during that summer, in a large room on the top floor of an old house on the North Side in Chicago. It was August and the night was hot. Until after midnight I sat—the sweat trickling down my back—under a lamp, laboring to feel my way into the lives of the fanciful people who were trying also to live in the tale on which I was at work.

It was a hopeless affair.

I became involved in the efforts of the shadowy people and they in turn became involved in the fact of the hot uncomfortable room, in the fact that, although it was what the farmers of the Middle West call "good corn-growing weather" it was plain hell to be alive in Chicago. Hand in hand the shadowy people of my fanciful world and myself groped our way through a forest in which the leaves had all been burned off the trees. The hot ground burned the shoes off our feet. We were striving to make our way through the forest and into some cool beautiful city. The fact is, as you will clearly understand, I was a little off my head.

When I gave up the struggle and got to my feet the chairs in the room danced about. They also were running aimlessly through a burning land and striving to reach some mythical city. "I'd better get out of here and go for a walk or go jump into the lake and cool myself off," I thought.

I went down out of my room and into the street. On a lower floor of the house lived two burlesque actresses who had just come in from their evening's work and who now sat in their room talking. As I reached the street something heavy whirled past my head and broke on the stone pavement. A white liquid spurted over my clothes and the voice of one of the actresses could be heard coming from the one lighted room of the house. "Oh, hell! We live such damned lives, we do, and we work in such a town! A dog is better off! And now they are going to take booze away from us too! I come home from working in that hot theatre on a hot night like this and what do I see—a half-filled bottle of spoiled milk standing on a window sill!

"I won't stand it! I got to smash everything!" she cried.

I walked eastward from my house. From the northwestern end of the city great hordes of men women and children had come to spend the night out of doors, by the shore of the lake. It was stifling hot there too and the air was heavy with a sense of struggle. On a few hundred acres of flat land, that had formerly been a swamp, some two million people were fighting for the peace and quiet of sleep and not getting it. Out of the half darkness, beyond the little strip of park land at the water's edge, the huge empty houses of Chicago's fashionable folk made a greyish-blue blot against the sky. "Thank the gods," I thought, "there are some people who can get out of here, who can go to the mountains or the seashore or to Europe." I stumbled in the half darkness over the legs of a woman who was lying and trying to sleep on the grass. A baby lay beside her and when she sat up it began to cry. I

muttered an apology and stepped aside and as I did so
my foot struck a half-filled milk bottle and I knocked it
over, the milk running out on the grass. "Oh, I'm sorry.
Please forgive me," I cried. "Never mind," the woman
answered, "the milk is sour."

He is a tall stooped-shouldered man with prematurely
greyed hair and works as a copy writer in an advertising
agency in Chicago—an agency where I also have sometimes been employed—and on that night in August I met
him, walking with quick eager strides along the shore of
the lake and past the tired petulant people. He did not
see me at first and I wondered at the evidence of life in
him when everyone else seemed half dead; but a street
lamp hanging over a nearby roadway threw its light down
upon my face and he pounced. "Here you, come up to my
place," he cried sharply. "I've got something to show you.
I was on my way down to see you. That's where I was
going," he lied as he hurried me along.

We went to his apartment on a street leading back from
the lake and the park. German, Polish, Italian and Jewish
families, equipped with soiled blankets and the ever-
present half-filled bottles of milk, had come prepared to
spend the night out of doors; but the American families
in the crowd were giving up the struggle to find a cool
spot and a little stream of them trickled along the
sidewalks, going back to hot beds in the hot houses.

It was past one o'clock and my friend's apartment was
disorderly as well as hot. He explained that his wife, with
their two children, had gone home to visit her mother on
a farm near Springfield, Illinois.

We took off our coats and sat down. My friend's thin
cheeks were flushed and his eyes shone. "You know—well
—you see," he began and then hesitated and laughed like

an embarrassed schoolboy. "Well now," he began again, "I've long been wanting to write something real, something besides advertisements. I suppose I'm silly but that's the way I am. It's been my dream to write something stirring and big. I suppose it's the dream of a lot of advertising writers, eh? Now look here — don't you go laughing. I think I've done it."

He explained that he had written something concerning Chicago, the capital and heart as he said, of the whole Central West. He grew angry. "People come here from the East or from farms, or from little holes of towns like I came from and they think it smart to run Chicago into the ground," he declared. "I thought I'd show 'em up," he added, jumping up and walking nervously about the room.

He handed me many sheets of paper covered with hastily scrawled words, but I protested and asked him to read it aloud. He did, standing with his face turned away from me. There was a quiver in his voice. The thing he had written concerned some mythical town I had never seen. He called it Chicago, but in the same breath spoke of great streets flaming with color, ghostlike buildings flung up into night skies and a river, running down a path of gold into the boundless West. It was the city, I told myself, I and the people of my story had been trying to find earlier on that same evening, when because of the heat I went a little off my head and could not work any more. The people of the city, he had written about, were a cool-headed, brave people, marching forward to some spiritual triumph, the promise of which was inherent in the physical aspects of the town.

Now I am one who, by the careful cultivation of certain traits in my character, have succeeded in building up the more brutal side of my nature, but I cannot knock

Chicago street-cars, nor can I tell an author to his face that I think his work is rotten.

"You're all right, Ed. You're great. You've knocked out a regular soc-dolager of a masterpiece here. Why you sound as good as Henry Mencken writing about Chicago as the literary centre of America, and you've lived in Chicago and he never did. The only thing I can see you've missed is a little something about the stockyards, and you can put that in later," I added and prepared to depart.

"What's this?" I asked, picking up a half-dozen sheets of paper that lay on the floor by my chair. I read it eagerly. And when I had finished reading it he stammered and apologized and then, stepping across the room, jerked the sheets out of my hand and threw them out at an open window. "I wish you hadn't seen that. It's something else I wrote about Chicago," he explained. He was flustered.

"You see the night was so hot, and, down at the office, I had to write a condensed-milk advertisement, just as I was sneaking away to come home and work on this other thing, and the street-car was so crowded and the people stank so, and when I finally got home here — the wife being gone—the place was a mess. Well, I couldn't write and I was sore. It's been my chance, you see, the wife and kids being gone and the house being quiet. I went for a walk. I think I went a little off my head. Then I came home and wrote that stuff I've just thrown out of the window."

He grew cheerful again. "Oh, well—it's all right. Writing that fool thing stirred me up and enabled me to write this other stuff, this real stuff I showed you first, about Chicago."

And so I went home and to bed, having in this odd way stumbled upon another bit of the kind of writing that is—

women and children down in order to get aboard
for better or worse — really presenting the lives of the
people of these towns and cities — sometimes in prose,
sometimes in stirring colorful song. It was the kind of
thing Mr. Sandburg or Mr. Masters might have done
after an evening's walk on a hot night in, say West Congress Street in Chicago.

The thing I had read of Ed's, centred about a half-
filled bottle of spoiled milk standing dim in the moonlight on a window sill. There had been a moon earlier on
that August evening, a new moon, a thin crescent golden
streak in the sky. What had happened to my friend, the
advertising writer, was something like this — I figured it
all out as I lay sleepless in bed after our talk.

I am sure I do not know whether or not it is true that all
advertising writers and newspaper men, want to do other
kinds of writing, but Ed did all right. The August day that
had preceded the hot night had been a hard one for him
to get through. All day he had been wanting to be at
home in his quiet apartment producing literature, rather
than sitting in an office and writing advertisements. In
the late afternoon, when he had thought his desk cleared
for the day, the boss of the copy writers came and ordered
him to write a page advertisement for the magazines on
the subject of condensed milk. "We got a chance to get a
new account if we can knock out some crackerjack stuff in
a hurry," he said. "I'm sorry to have to put it up to you on
such a rotten hot day, Ed, but we're up against it. Let's see
if you've got some of the old pep in you. Get down to
hardpan now and knock out something snappy and unusual before you go home."

Ed had tried. He put away the thoughts he had been
having about the city beautiful — the glowing city of the
plains — and got right down to business. He thought

about milk, milk or little children, the Chicagoans of the future, milk that would produce a little cream to put in the coffee of advertising writers in the morning, sweet fresh milk to keep all his brother and sister Chicagoans robust and strong. What Ed really wanted was a long cool drink of something with a kick in it, but he tried to make himself think he wanted a drink of milk. He gave himself over to thoughts of milk, milk condensed and yellow, milk warm from the cows his father owned when he was a boy —his mind launched a little boat and he set out on a sea of milk.

Out of it all he got what is called an original advertisement. The sea of milk on which he sailed became a mountain of cans of condensed milk, and out of that fancy he got his idea. He made a crude sketch for a picture showing wide rolling green fields with white farm houses. Cows grazed on the green hills and at one side of the picture a barefooted boy was driving a herd of Jersey cows out of the sweet fair land and down a lane into a kind of funnel at the small end of which was a tin of the condensed milk. Over the picture he put a heading: "The health and freshness of a whole countryside is condensed into one can of Whitney-Wells Condensed Milk." The head copy writer said it was a humdinger.

And then Ed went home. He wanted to begin writing about the city beautiful at once and so didn't go out to dinner, but fished about in the ice chest and found some cold meat out of which he made himself a sandwich. Also, he poured himself a glass of milk, but it was sour. "Oh, damn!" he said and poured it into the kitchen sink.

As Ed explained to me later, he sat down and tried to begin writing his real stuff at once, but he couldn't seem to get into it. The last hour in the office, the trip home in the hot smelly car, and the taste of the sour milk in his mouth had jangled his nerves. The truth is that Ed has a rather sensitive, finely balanced nature, and it had got mussed up.

He took a walk and tried to think, but his mind wouldn't stay where he wanted it to. Ed is now a man of nearly forty and on that night his mind ran back to his young manhood in the city, — and stayed there. Like other boys who had become grown men in Chicago, he had come to the city from a farm at the edge of a prairie town, and like all such town and farm boys, he had come filled with vague dreams.

What things he had hungered to do and be in Chicago! What he had done you can fancy. For one thing he had got himself married and now lived in the apartment on the North Side. To give a real picture of his life during the twelve or fifteen years that had slipped away since he was a young man would involve writing a novel, and that is not my purpose.

Anyway, there he was in his room—come home from his walk — and it was hot and quiet and he could not manage to get into his masterpiece. How still it was in the apartment with the wife and children away! His mind stayed on the subject of his youth in the city.

He remembered a night of his young manhood when he had gone out to walk, just as he did on that August evening. Then his life wasn't complicated by the fact of the wife and children and he lived alone in his room; but something had got on his nerves then, too. On that evening long ago he grew restless in his room and went out to walk. It was summer and first he went down by the river where ships were being loaded and then to a crowded park where girls and young fellows walked about.

He grew bold and spoke to a woman who sat alone on a park bench. She let him sit beside her and, because it was dark and she was silent, he began to talk. The night had made him sentimental. "Human beings are such hard things to get at. I wish I could get close to someone," he said. "Oh, you go on! What you doing? You ain't trying to kid someone?" asked the woman.

Ed jumped up and walked away. He went into a long street lined with dark silent buildings and then stopped and looked about. What he wanted was to believe that in the apartment buildings were people who lived intense eager lives, who had great dreams, who were capable of great adventures. "They are really only separated from me by the brick walls," was what he told himself on that night.

It was then that the milk bottle theme first got hold of him. He went into an alleyway to look at the backs of the apartment buildings and, on that evening also, there was a moon. Its light fell upon a long row of half-filled bottles standing on window sills.

Something within him went a little sick and he hurried out of the alleyway and into the street. A man and woman walked past him and stopped before the entrance to one of the buildings. Hoping they might be lovers, he concealed himself in the entrance to another building to listen to their conversation.

The couple turned out to be a man and wife and they were quarreling. Ed heard the woman's voice saying: "You come in here. You can't put that over on me. You say you just want to take a walk, but I know you. You want to go out and blow in some money. What I'd like to know is why you don't loosen up a little for me."

That is the story of what happened to Ed, when, as a young man, he went to walk in the city in the evening, and when he had become a man of forty and went out of his house wanting to dream and to think of a city beautiful, much the same sort of thing happened again. Perhaps the writing of the condensed milk advertisement and the taste of the sour milk he had got out of the ice box had something to do with his mood; but, anyway, milk bottles, like a refrain in a song, got into his brain. They seemed to sit and mock at him from the windows of all the buildings in all the streets, and when he turned to look at people, he met the crowds from the West and the Northwest Sides going to the park and the lake. At the head of each little group of people marched a woman who carried a milk bottle in her hand.

And so, on that August night, Ed went home angry and disturbed, and in anger wrote of his city. Like the burlesque actress in my own house he wanted to smash something, and, as milk bottles were in his mind, he wanted to smash milk bottles. "I could grasp the neck of a milk bottle. It fits the hand so neatly. I could kill a man or woman with such a thing," he thought desperately.

He wrote, you see, the five or six sheets I had read in that mood and then felt better. And after that he wrote about the ghostlike buildings flung into the sky by the hands of a brave adventurous people and about the river that runs down a path of gold, and into the boundless West.

As you have already concluded, the city he described in his masterpiece was lifeless, but the city he, in a queer way, expressed in what he wrote about the milk bottle could not be forgotten. It frightened you a little but there it was and in spite of his anger or perhaps because of it, a lovely singing quality had got into the thing. In those few scrawled pages the miracle had been worked. I was a fool not to have put the sheets into my pocket. When I went down out of his apartment that evening I did look for them in a dark alleyway, but they had become lost in a sea of rubbish that had leaked over the tops of a long row of tin ash cans that stood at the foot of a stairway leading from the back doors of the apartments above.

The Egg

M y father was, I am sure, intended by nature to be a cheerful, kindly man. Until he was thirty-four years old he worked as a farm-hand for a man named Thomas Butterworth whose place lay near the town of Bidwell, Ohio. He had then a horse of his own and on Saturday evenings drove into town to spend a few hours in social intercourse with other farm-hands. In town he drank several glasses of beer and stood about in Ben Head's saloon—crowded on Saturday evenings with visiting farm-hands. Songs were sung and glasses thumped on the bar. At ten o'clock father drove home along a lonely country road, made his horse comfortable for the night and himself went to bed, quite happy in his position in life. He had at that time no notion of trying to rise in the world.

It was in the spring of his thirty-fifth year that father married my mother, then a country school-teacher, and in the following spring I came wriggling and crying into the world. Something happened to the two people. They became ambitious. The American passion for getting up in the world took possession of them.

It may have been that mother was responsible. Being a school-teacher she had no doubt read books and magazines. She had, I presume, read of how Garfield, Lincoln, and other Americans rose from poverty to fame and greatness and as I lay beside her—in the days of her lying-in—she may have dreamed that I would some day rule men and cities. At any rate she induced father to give up his place as a farm-hand, sell his horse and embark on an independent enterprise of his own. She was a tall silent woman with a long nose and troubled grey eyes. For herself she wanted nothing. For father and myself she was incurably ambitious.

The first venture into which the two people went turned out badly. They rented ten acres of poor stony land on Grigg's Road, eight miles from Bidwell, and launched into chicken raising. I grew into boyhood on the place and got my first impressions of life there. From the beginning they were impressions of disaster and if, in my turn, I am a gloomy man inclined to see the darker side of life, I attribute it to the fact that what should have been for me the happy joyous days of childhood were spent on a chicken farm.

One unversed in such matters can have no notion of the many and tragic things that can happen to a chicken. It is born out of an egg, lives for a few weeks as a tiny fluffy thing such as you will see pictured on Easter cards, then becomes hideously naked, eats quantities of corn and meal bought by the sweat of your father's brow, gets diseases called pip, cholera, and other names, stands looking with stupid eyes at the sun, becomes sick and dies. A few hens and now and then a rooster, intended to serve God's mysterious ends, struggle through to maturity. The hens lay eggs out of which come other chickens and the dreadful cycle is thus made complete. It is all unbelievably complex. Most philosophers must have been raised on chicken farms. One hopes for so much from a chicken and is so dreadfully disillusioned. Small chickens, just setting out on the journey of life, look so bright and alert and they are in fact so dreadfully stupid. They are so much like people they mix one up in one's judgments of life. If disease does not kill them they wait until your expectations are thoroughly aroused and then walk under the wheels of a wagon—to go squashed and dead back to their maker. Vermin infest their youth, and fortunes must be spent for curative powders. In later life I have seen how a literature has been built up on the subject of fortunes to be made out of the raising of chickens. It is intended to be read by the gods who have just eaten of the tree of the knowledge of good and evil. It is a hopeful literature and declares that much may be done by simple ambitious people who own a few hens. Do not be led astray by it. It was not written for you. Go hunt for gold on the frozen hills of Alaska, put your faith in the honesty of a politician, believe if you will that the world is daily growing better and that good will triumph over evil, but do not read and believe the literature that is written concerning the hen. It was not written for you.

I, however, digress. My tale does not primarily concern itself with the hen. If correctly told it will centre on the egg. For ten years my father and mother struggled to make our chicken farm pay and then they gave up that struggle and began another. They moved into the town of Bidwell, Ohio and embarked in the restaurant business. After ten years of worry with incubators that did not hatch, and with tiny—and in their own way lovely—balls of fluff that passed on into semi-naked pullethood and from that into dead henhood, we threw all aside and packing our belongings on a wagon drove down Grigg's Road toward Bidwell, a tiny caravan of hope looking for a new place from which to start on our upward journey through life.

We must have been a sad looking lot, not, I fancy, unlike refugees fleeing from a battlefield. Mother and I walked in the road. The wagon that contained our goods had been borrowed for the day from Mr. Albert Griggs, a neighbor. Out of its sides stuck the legs of cheap chairs and at the back of the pile of beds, tables, and boxes filled with kitchen utensils was a crate of live chickens, and on top of that the baby carriage in which I had been wheeled about in my infancy. Why we stuck to the baby carriage I don't know. It was unlikely other children would be born and the wheels were broken. People who have few possessions cling tightly to those they have. That is one of the facts that make life so discouraging.

Father rode on top of the wagon. He was then a bald-headed man of forty-five, a little fat and from long association with mother and the chickens he had become habitually silent and discouraged. All during our ten years on the chicken farm he had worked as a laborer on neighboring farms and most of the money he had earned had been spent for remedies to cure chicken diseases, on Wilmer's White Wonder Cholera Cure or Professor Bidlow's Egg Producer or some other preparations that mother found advertised in the poultry papers. There were two little patches of hair on father's head just above his ears. I remember that as a child I used to sit looking at him when he had gone to sleep in a chair before the stove on Sunday afternoons in the winter. I had at that time already begun to read books and have notions of my own and the bald path that led over the top of his head was, I fancied, something like a broad road, such a road as Caesar might have made on which to lead his legions out of Rome and into the wonders of an unknown world. The tufts of hair that grew above father's ears were, I thought, like forests. I fell into a half-sleeping, half-waking state and dreamed I was a tiny thing going along the road into a far beautiful place where there were no chicken farms and where life was a happy eggless affair.

One might write a book concerning our flight from the chicken farm into town. Mother and I walked the entire eight miles — she to be sure that nothing fell from the wagon and I to see the wonders of the world. On the seat of the wagon beside father was his greatest treasure. I will tell you of that.

On a chicken farm where hundreds and even thousands of chickens come out of eggs surprising things sometimes happen. Grotesques are born out of eggs as out of people. The accident does not often occur — perhaps once in a thousand births. A chicken is, you see, born that has four legs, two pairs of wings, two heads or what not. The things do not live. They go quickly back to the hand of their maker that has for a moment trembled. The fact that the poor little things could not live was one of the tragedies of life to father. He had some sort of notion that if he could but bring into henhood or roosterhood a five-legged hen or a two-headed rooster his fortune would be made. He dreamed of taking the wonder about to county fairs and of growing rich by exhibiting it to other farm-hands.

At any rate he saved all the little monstrous things that had been born on our chicken farm. They were preserved in alcohol and put each in its own glass bottle. These he had carefully put into a box and on our journey into town it was carried on the wagon seat beside him. He drove the horses with one hand and with the other clung to the box. When we got to our destination the box was taken down at once and the bottles removed. All during our days as keepers of a restaurant in the town of Bidwell,

Ohio, the grotesques in their little glass bottles sat on a shelf back of the counter. Mother sometimes protested but father was a rock on the subject of his treasure. The grotesques were, he declared, valuable. People, he said, liked to look at strange and wonderful things.

Did I say that we embarked in the restaurant business in the town of Bidwell, Ohio? I exaggerated a little. The town itself lay at the foot of a low hill and on the shore of a small river. The railroad did not run through the town and the station was a mile away to the north at a place called Pickleville. There had been a cider mill and pickle factory at the station, but before the time of our coming they had both gone out of business. In the morning and in the evening busses came down to the station along a road called Turner's Pike from the hotel on the main street of Bidwell. Our going to the out of the way place to embark in the restaurant business was mother's idea. She talked of it for a year and then one day went off and rented an empty store building opposite the railroad station. It was her idea that the restaurant would be profitable. Travelling men, she said, would be always waiting around to take trains out of town and town people would come to the station to await incoming trains. They would come to the restaurant to buy pieces of pie and drink coffee. Now that I am older I know that she had another motive in going. She was ambitious for me. She wanted me to rise in the world, to get into a town school and become a man of the towns.

At Pickleville father and mother worked hard as they always had done. At first there was the necessity of putting our place into shape to be a restaurant. That took a month. Father built a shelf on which he put tins of vegetables. He painted a sign on which he put his name in large red letters. Below his name was the sharp command

— "EAT HERE" — that was so seldom obeyed. A show case was bought and filled with cigars and tobacco. Mother scrubbed the floor and the walls of the room. I went to school in the town and was glad to be away from the farm and from the presence of the discouraged, sad-looking chickens. Still I was not very joyous. In the evening I walked home from school along Turner's Pike and remembered the children I had seen playing in the town school yard. A troop of little girls had gone hopping about and singing. I tried that. Down along the frozen road I went hopping solemnly on one leg. "Hippity Hop To The Barber Shop," I sang shrilly. Then I stopped and looked doubtfully about. I was afraid of being seen in my gay mood. It must have seemed to me that I was doing a thing that should not be done by one who, like myself, had been raised on a chicken farm where death was a daily visitor.

Mother decided that our restaurant should remain open at night. At ten in the evening a passenger train went north past our door followed by a local freight. The freight crew had switching to do in Pickleville and when the work was done they came to our restaurant for hot coffee and food. Sometimes one of them ordered a fried egg. In the morning at four they returned north-bound and again visited us. A little trade began to grow up. Mother slept at night and during the day tended the restaurant and fed our boarders while father slept. He slept in the same bed mother had occupied during the night and I went off to the town of Bidwell and to school. During the long nights, while mother and I slept, father cooked meats that were to go into sandwiches for the lunch baskets of our boarders. Then an idea in regard to getting up in the world came into to his head. The American spirit took hold of him. He also became ambitious.

In the long nights when there was little to do father had time to think. That was his undoing. He decided that he had in the past been an unsuccessful man because he had not been cheerful enough and that in the future he would adopt a cheerful outlook on life. In the early morning he came upstairs and got into bed with mother. She woke and the two talked. From my bed in the corner I listened.

It was father's idea that both he and mother should try to entertain the people who came to eat at our restaurant. I cannot now remember his words, but he gave the impression of one about to become in some obscure way a kind of public entertainer. When people, particularly young people from the town of Bidwell, came into our place, as on very rare occasions they did, bright entertaining conversation was to be made. From father's words I gathered that something of the jolly inn-keeper effect was to be sought. Mother must have been doubtful from the first, but she said nothing discouraging. It was father's notion that a passion for the company of himself and mother would spring up in the breasts of the younger people of the town of Bidwell. In the evening bright happy groups would come singing down Turner's Pike. They would troop shouting with joy and laughter into our place. There would be song and festivity. I do not mean to give the impression that father spoke so elaborately of the matter. He was as I have said an uncommunicative man. "They want some place to go. I tell you they want some place to go," he said over and over. That was as far as he got. My own imagination has filled in the blanks.

For two or three weeks this notion of father's invaded our house. We did not talk much, but in our daily lives tried earnestly to make smiles take the place of glum looks. Mother smiled at the boarders and I, catching the infection, smiled at our cat. Father became a little feverish in his anxiety to please. There was no doubt, lurking somewhere in him, a touch of the spirit of the showman. He did not waste much of his ammunition on the railroad men he served at night but seemed to be waiting for a young man or woman from Bidwell to come in to show what he could do. On the counter in the restaurant there was a wire basket kept always filled with eggs, and it must have been before his eyes when the idea of being entertaining was born in his brain. There was something pre-natal about the way eggs kept themselves connected with the development of his idea. At any rate an egg ruined his new impulse in life. Late one night I was awakened by a roar of anger coming from father's throat. Both mother and I sat upright in our beds. With trembling hands she lighted a lamp that stood on a table by her head. Downstairs the front door of our restaurant went shut with a bang and in a few minutes father tramped up the stairs. He held an egg in his hand and his hand trembled as though he were having a chill. There was a half insane light in his eyes. As he stood glaring at us I was sure he intended throwing the egg at either mother or me. Then he laid it gently on the table beside the lamp and dropped on his knees beside mother's bed. He began to cry like a boy and I, carried away by his grief, cried with him. The two of us filled the little upstairs room with our wailing voices. It is ridiculous, but of the picture we made I can remember only the fact that mother's hand continually stroked the bald path that ran across the top of his head. I have forgotten what mother said to him and how she induced him to tell her of what had happened downstairs. His explanation also has gone out of my mind. I remember only my own grief and fright and the shiny path over father's head glowing in the lamp light as he knelt by the bed.

As to what happened downstairs. For some unexplainable reason I know the story as well as though I had been a witness to my father's discomfiture. One in time gets to know many unexplainable things. On that evening young Joe Kane, son of a merchant of Bidwell, came to Pickleville to meet his father, who was expected on the ten o'clock evening train from the South. The train was three hours late and Joe came into our place to loaf about and to wait for its arrival. The local freight train came in and the freight crew were fed. Joe was left alone in the restaurant with father.

From the moment he came into our place the Bidwell young man must have been puzzled by my father's actions. It was his notion that father was angry at him for hanging around. He noticed that the restaurant keeper was apparently disturbed by his presence and he thought of going out. However, it began to rain and he did not fancy the long walk to town and back. He bought a five-cent cigar and ordered a cup of coffee. He had a newspaper in his pocket and took it out and began to read. "I'm waiting for the evening train. It's late," he said apologetically.

For a long time father, whom Joe Kane had never seen before, remained silently gazing at his visitor. He was no doubt suffering from an attack of stage fright. As so often happens in life he had thought so much and so often of the situation that now confronted him that he was somewhat nervous in its presence.

For one thing, he did not know what to do with his hands. He thrust one of them nervously over the counter and shook hands with Joe Kane. "How-de-do," he said. Joe Kane put his newspaper down and stared at him. Father's eye lighted on the basket of eggs that sat on the counter and he began to talk. "Well," he began hesitatingly, "well, you have heard of Christopher Columbus,

eh?" He seemed to be angry. "That Christopher Columbus was a cheat," he declared emphatically. "He talked of
making an egg stand on its end. He talked, he did, and
then he went and broke the end of the egg."

My father seemed to his visitor to be beside himself at
the duplicity of Christopher Columbus. He muttered
and swore. He declared it was wrong to teach children
that Christopher Columbus was a great man when, after
all, he cheated at the critical moment. He had declared he
would make an egg stand on end and then when his bluff
had been called he had done a trick. Still grumbling at
Columbus, father took an egg from the basket on the
counter and began to walk up and down. He rolled the
egg between the palms of his hands. He smiled genially.
He began to mumble words regarding the effect to be
produced on an egg by the electricity that comes out of
the human body. He declared that without breaking its
shell and by virtue of rolling it back and forth in his hands
he could stand the egg on its end. He explained that the
warmth of his hands and the gentle rolling movement he
gave the egg created a new centre of gravity, and Joe
Kane was mildly interested. "I have handled thousands
of eggs," father said. "No one knows more about eggs
than I do."

He stood the egg on the counter and it fell on its side.
He tried the trick again and again, each time rolling the
egg between the palms of his hands and saying the words
regarding the wonders of electricity and the laws of gravity. When after a half hour's effort he did succeed in
making the egg stand for a moment he looked up to find
his visitor was no longer watching. By the time he had
succeeded in calling Joe Kane's attention to the success of
his effort the egg had again rolled over and lay on its side.

Afire with the showman's passion and at the same time

a good deal disconcerted by the failure of his first effort, father now took the bottles containing the poultry monstrosities down from their place on the shelf and began to show them to his visitor. "How would you like to have seven legs and two heads like this fellow?" he asked, exhibiting the most remarkable of his treasures. A cheerful smile played over his face. He reached over the counter and tried to slap Joe Kane on the shoulder as he had seen men do in Ben Head's saloon when he was a young farm-hand and drove to town on Saturday evenings. His visitor was made a little ill by the sight of the body of the terribly deformed bird floating in the alcohol in the bottle and got up to go. Coming from behind the counter father took hold of the young man's arm and led him back to his seat. He grew a little angry and for a moment had to turn his face away and force himself to smile. Then he put the bottles back on the shelf. In an outburst of generosity he fairly compelled Joe Kane to have a fresh cup of coffee and another cigar at his expense. Then he took a pan and filling it with vinegar, taken from a jug that sat beneath the counter, he declared himself about to do a new trick. "I will heat this egg in this pan of vinegar," he said. "Then I will put it through the neck of a bottle without breaking the shell. When the egg is inside the bottle it will resume its normal shape and the shell will become hard again. Then I will give the bottle with the egg in it to you. You can take it about with you wherever you go. People will want to know how you got the egg in the bottle. Don't tell them. Keep them guessing. That is the way to have fun with this trick."

Father grinned and winked at his visitor. Joe Kane decided that the man who confronted him was mildly insane but harmless. He drank the cup of coffee that had been given him and began to read his paper again. When the egg had been heated in vinegar father carried it on a spoon to the counter and going into a back room got an empty bottle. He was angry because his visitor did not watch him as he began to do his trick, but nevertheless went cheerfully to work. For a long time he struggled, trying to get the egg to go through the neck of the bottle. He put the pan of vinegar back on the stove, intending to reheat the egg, then picked it up and burned his fingers. After a second bath in the hot vinegar the shell of the egg had been softened a little but not enough for his purpose. He worked and worked and a spirit of desperate determination took possession of him. When he thought that at last the trick was about to be consummated the delayed train came in at the station and Joe Kane started to go nonchalantly out at the door. Father made a last desperate effort to conquer the egg and make it do the thing that would establish his reputation as one who knew how to entertain guests who came into his restaurant. He worried the egg. He attempted to be somewhat rough with it. He swore and the sweat stood out on his forehead. The egg broke under his hand. When the contents spurted over his clothes, Joe Kane, who had stopped at the door, turned and laughed.

A roar of anger rose from my father's throat. He danced and shouted a string of inarticulate words. Grabbing another egg from the basket on the counter, he threw it, just missing the head of the young man as he dodged through the door and escaped.

Father came upstairs to mother and me with an egg in his hand. I do not know what he intended to do. I imagine he had some idea of destroying it, of destroying all eggs, and that he intended to let mother and me see him begin. When, however, he got into the presence of mother something happened to him. He laid the egg gently on the table and dropped on his knees by the bed as I have already explained. He later decided to close the restaurant for the night and to come upstairs and get into bed. When he did so he blew out the light and after much muttered conversation both he and mother went to sleep. I suppose I went to sleep also, but my sleep was troubled. I awoke at dawn and for a long time looked at the egg that lay on the table. I wondered why eggs had to be and why from the egg came the hen who again laid the egg. The question got into my blood. It has stayed there, I imagine, because I am the son of my father. At any rate, the problem remains unsolved in my mind. And that, I conclude, is but another evidence of the complete and final triumph of the egg — at least as far as my family is concerned.

The Man
Who Became a Woman

My father was a retail druggist in our town, out in
Nebraska, which was so much like a thousand
other towns I've been in since that there's no use fooling
around and taking up your time and mine trying to
describe it.

Anyway I became a drug clerk and after father's death
the store was sold and mother took the money and went
west, to her sister in California, giving me four hundred
dollars with which to make my start in the world. I was
only nineteen years old then.

I came to Chicago, where I worked as a drug clerk for a
time, and then, as my health suddenly went back on me,
perhaps because I was so sick of my lonely life in the city
and of the sight and smell of the drug store, I decided to
set out on what seemed to me then the great adventure
and became for a time a tramp, working now and then,
when I had no money, but spending all the time I could
loafing around out of doors or riding up and down the
land on freight trains and trying to see the world. I even
did some stealing in lonely towns at night—once a pretty
good suit of clothes that someone had left hanging out on
a clothesline, and once some shoes out of a box in a
freight car—but I was in constant terror of being caught

and put into jail so I realized that success as a thief was not for me.

The most delightful experience of that period of my life was when I once worked as a groom, or swipe, with race horses and it was during that time I met a young fellow of about my own age who has since become a writer of some prominence.

The young man of whom I now speak had gone into race track work as a groom, to bring a kind of flourish, a high spot, he used to say, into his life.

He was then unmarried and had not been successful as a writer. What I mean is he was free and I guess, with him as with me, there was something he liked about the people who hang about a race track, the touts, swipes, drivers, niggers and gamblers. You know what a gaudy undependable lot they are—if you've ever been around the tracks much—about the best liars I've ever seen, and not saving money or thinking about morals, like most druggists, dry-goods merchants and the others who used to be my father's friends in our Nebraska town—and not bending the knee much either, or kowtowing to people, they thought must be grander or richer or more power-ful than themselves.

What I mean is, they were an independent, go-to-the-devil, come-have-a-drink-of-whisky, kind of a crew and when one of them won a bet, "knocked 'em off," we called it, his money was just dirt to him while it lasted. No king or president or soap manufacturer—gone on a trip with his family to Europe—could throw on more dog than one of them, with his big diamond rings and the diamond horse-shoe stuck in his necktie and all.

I liked the whole blamed lot pretty well and he did too.

He was groom temporarily for a pacing gelding named Lumpy Joe owned by a tall black-mustached man named

Alfred Kreymborg and trying the best he could to make
the bluff to himself he was a real one. It happened that we
were on the same circuit, doing the West Pennsylvania
county fairs all that fall, and on fine evenings we spent a
good deal of time walking and talking together.

Let us suppose it to be a Monday or Tuesday evening
and our horses had been put away for the night. The
racing didn't start until later in the week, maybe Wednesday, usually. There was always a little place called a
dining-hall, run mostly by the Woman's Christian Tem-
perance Associations of the towns, and we would go there
to eat where we could get a pretty good meal for twenty-
five cents. At least then we thought it pretty good.

I would manage it so that I sat beside this fellow, whose
name was Tom Means and when we had got through
eating we would go look at our two horses again and
when we got there Lumpy Joe would be eating his hay in
his box stall and Alfred Kreymborg would be standing
there, pulling his mustache and looking as sad as a sick
crane.

But he wasn't really sad. "You two boys want to go down
town to see the girls. I'm an old duffer and way past that
myself. You go on along. I'll be setting here anyway, and
I'll keep an eye on both the horses for you," he would say.

So we would set off, going, not into the town to try to
get in with some of the town girls, who might have taken
up with us because we were strangers and race track
fellows, but out into the country. Sometimes we got into a
hilly country and there was a moon. The leaves were
falling off the trees and lay in the road so that we kicked
them up with the dust as we went along.

To tell the truth I suppose I got to love Tom Means,
who was five years older than me, although I wouldn't
have dared say so, then. Americans are shy and timid

about saying things like that and a man here don't dare own up he loves another man, I've found out, and they are afraid to admit such feelings to themselves even. I guess they're afraid it may be taken to mean something it don't need to at all.

Anyway we walked along and some of the trees were already bare and looked like people standing solemnly beside the road and listening to what we had to say. Only I didn't say much. Tom Means did most of the talking.

Sometimes we came back to the race track and it was late and the moon had gone down and it was dark. Then we often walked round and round the track, sometimes a dozen times, before we crawled into the hay to go to bed.

Tom talked always on two subjects, writing and race horses, but mostly about race horses. The quiet sounds about the race tracks and the smells of horses, and the things that go with horses, seemed to get him all excited. "Oh, hell, Herman Dudley," he would burst out suddenly, "don't go talking to me. I know what I think. I've been around more than you have and I've seen a world of people. There isn't any man or woman, not even a fellow's own mother, as fine as a horse, that is to say a thoroughbred horse."

Sometimes he would go on like that a long time, speaking of people he had seen and their characteristics. He wanted to be a writer later and what he said was that when he came to be one he wanted to write the way a well bred horse runs or trots or paces. Whether he ever did it or not I can't say. He has written a lot, but I'm not too good a judge of such things. Anyway I don't think he has.

But when he got on the subject of horses he certainly was a darby. I would never have felt the way I finally got to feel about horses or enjoyed my stay among them half so much if it hadn't been for him. Often he would go on talking for an hour maybe, speaking of horses' bodies and of their minds and wills as though they were human beings. "Lord help us, Herman," he would say, grabbing hold of my arm, "don't it get you up in the throat? I say now, when a good one, like that Lumpy Joe I'm swiping, flattens himself at the head of the stretch and he's coming, and you know he's coming, and you know his heart's sound and he's game, and you know he isn't going to let himself get licked—don't it get you Herman, don't it get you like the old Harry?"

That's the way he would talk, and then later, sometimes, he'd talk about writing and get himself all het up about that too. He had some notions about writing I've never got myself around to thinking much about but just the same maybe his talk, working in me, has led me to want to begin to write this story myself.

There was one experience of that time on the tracks that I am forced, by some feeling inside myself, to tell.

Well, I don't know why but I've just got to. It will be kind of like confession is, I suppose, to a good Catholic, or maybe, better yet, like cleaning up the room you live in, if you are a bachelor, like I was for so long. The room gets pretty mussy and the bed not made some days and clothes and things thrown on the closet floor and maybe under the bed. And then you clean all up and put on new sheets, and then you take off all your clothes and get down on your hands and knees, and scrub the floor so clean you could eat bread off it, and then take a walk and come home after a while and your room smells sweet and you feel sweetened-up and better inside yourself too.

What I mean is, this story has been on my chest, and I've often dreamed about the happenings in it, even after I married Jessie and was happy. Sometimes I even screamed out at night and so I said to myself, "I'll write the dang story," and here goes.

Fall had come on and in the mornings now when we crept out of our blankets, spread out on the hay in the tiny lofts above the horse stalls, and put our heads out to look around, there was a white rime of frost on the ground. When we woke the horses woke too. You know how it is at the tracks — the little barn-like stalls with the tiny lofts above are all set along in a row and there are two doors to each stall, one coming up to a horse's breast and then a top one, that is only closed at night and in bad weather.

In the mornings the upper door is swung open and fastened back and the horses put their heads out. There is the white rime on the grass over inside the grey oval the track makes. Usually there is some outfit that has six, ten or even twelve horses, and perhaps they have a negro cook who does his cooking at an open fire in the clear space before the row of stalls and he is at work now and the horses with their big fine eyes are looking about and whinnying, and a stallion looks out at the door of one of the stalls and sees a sweet-eyed mare looking at him and sends up his trumpet-call, and a man's voice laughs, and there are no women anywhere in sight or no sign of one anywhere, and everyone feels like laughing and usually does.

It's pretty fine but I didn't know how fine it was until I got to know Tom Means and heard him talk about it all.

At the time the thing happened of which I am trying to tell now Tom was no longer with me. A week before his owner, Alfred Kreymborg, had taken his horse Lumpy Joe over into the Ohio Fair Circuit and I saw no more of Tom at the tracks.

There was a story going about the stalls that Lumpy

Joe, a big rangy brown gelding, wasn't really named Lumpy Joe at all, that he was a ringer who had made a fast record out in Iowa and up through the northwest country the year before, and that Kreymborg had picked him up and had kept him under wraps all winter and had brought him over into the Pennsylvania country under this new name and made a clean-up in the books.

I know nothing about that and never talked to Tom about it but anyway he, Lumpy Joe and Kreymborg were all gone now.

I suppose I'll always remember those days, and Tom's talk at night, and before that in the early September evenings how we sat around in front of the stalls, and Kreymborg sitting on an upturned feed box and pulling at his long black mustache and sometimes humming a little ditty one couldn't catch the words of. It was something about a deep well and a little grey squirrel crawling up the sides of it, and he never laughed or smiled much but there was something in his solemn grey eyes, not quite a twinkle, something more delicate than that.

The others talked in low tones and Tom and I sat in silence. He never did his best talking except when he and I were alone.

For his sake — if he ever sees my story — I should mention that at the only big track we ever visited, at Readville, Pennsylvania, we saw old Pop Geers, the great racing driver, himself. His horses were at a place far away across the tracks from where we were stabled. I suppose a man like him was likely to get the choice of all the good places for his horses.

We went over there one evening and stood about and there was Geers himself, sitting before one of the stalls on a box tapping the ground with a riding whip. They called him, around the tracks, "The silent man from Tennessee" and he was silent—that night anyway. All we did was to stand and look at him for maybe a half hour and then we went away and that night Tom talked better than I had ever heard him. He said that the ambition of his life was to wait until Pop Geers died and then write a book about him, and to show in the book that there was at least one American who never went nutty about getting rich or owning a big factory or being any other kind of a hell of a fellow. "He's satisfied I think to sit around like that and wait until the big moments of his life come, when he heads a fast one into the stretch and then, darn his soul, he can give all of himself to the thing right in front of him," Tom said, and then he was so worked up he began to blubber. We were walking along the fence on the inside of the tracks and it was dusk and, in some trees nearby, some birds, just sparrows maybe, were making a chirping sound, and you could hear insects singing and, where there was a little light, off to the west between some trees, motes were dancing in the air. Tom said that about Pop Geers, although I think he was thinking most about something he wanted to be himself and wasn't, and then he went and stood by the fence and sort of blubbered and I began to blubber too, although I didn't know what about.

But perhaps I did know, after all. I suppose Tom wanted to feel, when he became a writer, like he thought old Pop must feel when his horse swung around the upper turn, and there lay the stretch before him, and if he was going to get his horse home in front he had to do it right then. What Tom said was that any man had something in him that understands about a thing like that but that no woman ever did except up in her brain. He often got off things like that about women but I notice he later married one of them just the same.

But to get back to my knitting. After Tom had left, the stable I was with kept drifting along through nice little Pennsylvania county seat towns. My owner, a strange excitable kind of a man from over in Ohio, who had lost a lot of money on horses but was always thinking he would maybe get it all back in some big killing, had been playing in pretty good luck that year. The horse I had, a tough little gelding, a five year old, had been getting home in front pretty regular and so he took some of his winnings and bought a three years old black pacing stallion named "O, My Man." My gelding was called "Pick-it-boy" because when he was in a race and had got into the stretch my owner always got half wild with excitement and shouted so you could hear him a mile and a half. "Go, pick it boy, pick it boy, pick it boy," he kept shouting and so when he had got hold of this good little gelding he had named him that.

The gelding was a fast one, all right. As the boys at the tracks used to say, he "picked 'em up sharp and set 'em down clean," and he was what we called a natural race horse, right up to all the speed he had, and didn't require much training. "All you got to do is to drop him down on the track and he'll go," was what my owner was always saying to other men, when he was bragging about his horse.

And so you see, after Tom left, I hadn't much to do evenings and then the new stallion, the three year old, came on with a negro swipe named Burt.

I liked him fine and he liked me but not the same as Tom and me. We got to be friends all right and I suppose Burt would have done things for me, and maybe me for him, that Tom and me wouldn't have done for each other.

But with a negro you couldn't be close friends like you can with another white man. There's some reason you can't understand but it's true. There's been too much talk about the difference between whites and blacks and you're both shy, and anyway no use trying and I suppose Burt and I both knew it and so I was pretty lonesome.

Something happened to me that happened several times, when I was a young fellow, that I have never exactly understood. Sometimes now I think it was all because I had got to be almost a man and had never been with a woman. I don't know what's the matter with me. I can't ask a woman. I've tried it a good many times in my life but every time I've tried the same thing happened.

Of course, with Jessie now, it's different, but at the time of which I'm speaking Jessie was a long ways off and a good many things were to happen to me before I got to her.

Around a race track, as you may suppose, the fellows who are swipes and drivers and strangers in the towns do not go without women. They don't have to. In any town there are always some fly girls will come around a place like that. I suppose they think they are fooling with men who lead romantic lives. Such girls will come along by the front of the stalls where the race horses are and, if you look all right to them, they will stop and make a fuss over your horse. They rub their little hands over the horse's nose and then is the time for you—if you aren't a fellow like me who can't get up the nerve—then is the time for you to smile and say, "Hello, kid," and then make a date with one of them for that evening up town after supper. I couldn't do that, although the Lord knows I tried hard enough, often enough. A girl would come along alone, and she would be a little thing and give me the eye, and I would try and try but couldn't say anything. Both Tom, and Burt afterwards, used to laugh at me about it sometimes but what I think is that, had I been able to speak up to one of them and had managed to make a date with her, nothing would have come of it. We would probably have walked around the town and got off together in the dark somewhere, where the town came to an end, and then she would have had to knock me over with a club before it got any further.

And so there I was, having got used to Tom and our talks together, and Burt of course had his own friends among the black men. I got lazy and mopey and had a hard time doing my work.

It was like this. Sometimes I would be sitting, perhaps under a tree in the late afternoon when the races were over for the day and the crowds had gone away. There were always a lot of other men and boys who hadn't any horses in the races that day and they would be standing or sitting about in front of the stalls and talking.

I would listen for a time to their talk and then their voices would seem to go far away. The things I was look-ing at would go far away too. Perhaps there would be a tree, not more than a hundred yards away, and it would just come out of the ground and float away like a thistle. It would get smaller and smaller, away off there in the sky, and then suddenly — bang, it would be back where it belonged, in the ground, and I would begin hearing the voices of the men talking again.

When Tom was with me that summer the nights were splendid. We usually walked about and talked until pretty late and then I crawled up into my hole and went to sleep. Always out of Tom's talk I got something that stayed in my mind, after I was off by myself, curled up in my blanket. I suppose he had a way of making pictures as he talked and the pictures stayed by me as Burt was always saying pork chops did by him. "Give me the old pork chops, they stick to the ribs," Burt was always saying and with the imagination it was always that way about Tom's talks. He started something inside you that went on and on, and your mind played with it like walking about in a strange town and seeing the sights, and you slipped off to sleep and had splendid dreams and woke up in the morning feeling fine.

And then he was gone and it wasn't that way any more and I got into the fix I have described. At night I kept seeing women's bodies and women's lips and things in my dreams, and woke up in the morning feeling like the old Harry.

Burt was pretty good to me. He always helped me cool Pick-it-boy out after a race and he did the things himself that take the most skill and quickness, like getting the bandages on a horse's leg smooth, and seeing that every strap is setting just right, and every buckle drawn up to just the right hole, before your horse goes out on the track for a heat.

Burt knew there was something wrong with me and put himself out not to let the boss know. When the boss was around he was always bragging about me. "The brightest kid I've ever worked with around the tracks," he would say and grin, and that at a time when I wasn't worth my salt.

When you go out with the horses there is one job that always takes a lot of time. In the late afternoon, after your horse has been in a race and after you have washed him and rubbed him out, he has to be walked slowly, sometimes for hours and hours, so he'll cool out slowly and won't get muscle-bound. I got so I did that job for both our horses and Burt did the more important things. It left him free to go talk or shoot dice with the other niggers and I didn't mind. I rather liked it and after a hard race even the stallion, O My Man, was tame enough, even when there were mares about.

You walk and walk and walk, around a little circle, and your horse's head is right by your shoulder, and all around you the life of the place you are in is going on, and in a queer way you get so you aren't really a part of it at all. Perhaps no one ever gets as I was then, except boys that aren't quite men yet and who like me have never been with girls or women—to really be with them, up to the hilt, I mean. I used to wonder if young girls got that way too before they married or did what we used to call "go on the town."

If I remember it right though, I didn't do much thinking then. Often I would have forgotten supper if Burt hadn't shouted at me and reminded me, and sometimes he forgot and went off to town with one of the other niggers and I did forget.

There I was with the horse, going slow slow slow, around a circle that way. The people were leaving the fair grounds now, some afoot, some driving away to the farms in wagons and fords. Clouds of dust floated in the air and over to the west, where the town was, maybe the sun was going down, a red ball of fire through the dust. Only a few hours before the crowd had been all filled with excitement and everyone shouting. Let us suppose my horse had been in a race that afternoon and I had stood in front of the grandstand with my horse blanket over my shoulder, alongside of Burt perhaps, and when they came into the stretch my owner began to call, in that queer high voice of his that seemed to float over the top of all the shouting up in the grandstand. And his voice was saying over and over, "Go, pick it boy, pick it boy, pick it boy," the way he always did, and my heart was thumping so I could hardly breathe, and Burt was leaning over and snapping his fingers and muttering, "Come, little sweet.

Come on home. Your Mama wants you. Come get your 'lasses and bread, little Pick-it-boy."

Well, all that was over now and the voices of the people left around were all low. And Pick-it-boy—I was leading him slowly around the little ring, to cool him out slowly, as I've said, — he was different too. Maybe he had pretty nearly broken his heart trying to get down to the wire in front, or getting down there in front, and now everything inside him was quiet and tired, as it was nearly all the time those days in me, except in me tired but not quiet.

You remember I've told you we always walked in a circle; round and round and round. I guess something inside me got to going round and round and round too. The sun did sometimes and the trees and the clouds of dust. I had to think sometimes about putting down my feet so they went down in the right place and I didn't get to staggering like a drunken man.

And a funny feeling came that it is going to be hard to describe. It had something to do with the life in the horse and in me. Sometimes, these late years, I've thought maybe negroes would understand what I'm trying to talk about now better than any white man ever will. I mean something about men and animals, something between them, something that can perhaps only happen to a white man when he has slipped off his base a little, as I suppose I had then. I think maybe a lot of horsey people feel it sometimes though. It's something like this, maybe—do you suppose it could be that something we whites have got, and think such a lot of, and are so proud about, isn't much of any good after all?

It's something in us that wants to be big and grand and important maybe and won't let us just be, like a horse or a dog or a bird can. Let's say Pick-it-boy had won his race that day. He did that pretty often that summer. Well, he was neither proud, like I would have been in his place, or mean in one part of the inside of him either. He was just himself, doing something with a kind of simplicity. That's what Pick-it-boy was like and I got to feeling it in him as I walked with him slowly in the gathering darkness. I got inside him in some way I can't explain and he got inside me. Often we would stop walking for no cause and he would put his nose up against my face.

I wished he was a girl sometimes or that I was a girl and he was a man. It's an odd thing to say but it's a fact. Being with him that way, so long, and in such a quiet way, cured something in me a little. Often after an evening like that I slept all right and did not have the kind of dreams I've spoken about.

But I wasn't cured for very long and couldn't get cured. My body seemed all right and just as good as ever, but there wasn't no pep in me.

Then the fall got later and later and we came to the last town we were going to make before my owner laid his horses up for the winter, in his home town over across the State line in Ohio, and the track was up on a hill, or rather in a kind of high plain above the town.

It wasn't much of a place and the sheds were rather rickety and the track bad, especially at the turns. As soon as we got to the place and got stabled it began to rain and kept it up all week so the fair had to be put off.

As the purses weren't very large a lot of the owners shipped right out but our owner stayed. The fair owners guaranteed expenses, whether the races were held the next week or not.

And all week there wasn't much of anything for Burt and me to do but clean manure out of the stalls in the morning, watch for a chance when the rain let up a little to jog the horses around the track in the mud and then clean them off, blanket them and stick them back in their stalls.

It was the hardest time of all for me. Burt wasn't so bad off as there were a dozen or two blacks around and in the evening they went off to town, got liquored up a little and came home late, singing and talking, even in the cold rain.

And then one night I got mixed up in the thing I'm trying to tell you about.

It was a Saturday evening and when I look back at it now it seems to me everyone had left the tracks but just me. In the early evening swipe after swipe came over to my stall and asked me if I was going to stick around. When I said I was he would ask me to keep an eye out for him, that nothing happened to his horse. "Just take a stroll down that way now and then, eh, kid," one of them would say, "I just want to run up to town for an hour or two."

I would say "yes" to be sure, and so pretty soon it was dark as pitch up there in that little ruined fairground and nothing living anywhere around but the horses and me.

I stood it as long as I could, walking here and there in the mud and rain, and thinking all the time I wished I was someone else and not myself. "If I were someone else," I thought, "I wouldn't be here but down there in town with the others." I saw myself going into saloons and having drinks and later going off to a house maybe and getting myself a woman.

I got to thinking so much that, as I went stumbling around up there in the darkness, it was as though what was in my mind was actually happening.

Only I wasn't with some cheap woman, such as I would have found had I had the nerve to do what I wanted but with such a woman as I thought then I should never find in this world. She was slender and like a flower and with something in her like a race horse too, something in her like Pick-it-boy in the stretch, I guess.

And I thought about her and thought about her until I couldn't stand thinking any more. "I'll do something anyway," I said to myself.

So, although I had told all the swipes I would stay and watch their horses, I went out of the fair grounds and down the hill a ways. I went down until I came to a little low saloon, not in the main part of the town itself but half way up the hillside. The saloon had once been a residence, a farmhouse perhaps, but if it was ever a farmhouse I'm sure the farmer who lived there and worked the land on that hillside hadn't made out very well. The country didn't look like a farming country, such as one sees all about the other county-seat towns we had been visiting all through the late summer and fall. Everywhere you looked there were stones sticking out of the ground and the trees mostly of the stubby, stunted kind. It looked wild and untidy and ragged, that's what I mean. On the flat plain, up above, where the fairground was, there were a few fields and pastures, and there were some sheep raised and in the field right next to the tracks, on the furtherest side from town, on the back stretch side, there had once been a slaughter-house, the ruins of which were still standing. It hadn't been used for quite some time but there were bones of animals lying all about in the field, and there was a smell coming out of the old building that would curl your hair.

The horses hated the place, just as we swipes did, and in the morning when we were jogging them around the track in the mud, to keep them in racing condition, Pick-it-boy and O My Man both raised old Ned every time we headed them up the back stretch and got near to where the old slaughter-house stood. They would rear and fight at the bit, and go off their stride and run until they got clear of the rotten smells, and neither Burt nor I could make them stop it. "It's a hell of a town down there and this is a hell of a track for racing," Burt kept saying. "If they ever have their danged old fair someone's going to get spilled and maybe killed back here." Whether they did or not I don't know as I didn't stay for the fair, for reasons I'll tell you pretty soon, but Burt was speaking sense all right. A race horse isn't like a human being. He won't stand for it to have to do his work in any rotten ugly kind of a dump the way a man will, and he won't stand for the smells a man will either.

But to get back to my story again. There I was, going down the hillside in the darkness and the cold soaking rain and breaking my word to all the others about staying up above and watching the horses. When I got to the little saloon I decided to stop and have a drink or two. I'd found out long before that about two drinks upset me so I was two-thirds piped and couldn't walk straight, but on that night I didn't care a tinker's dam.

So I went up a kind of path, out of the road, toward the front door of the saloon. It was in what must have been the parlor of the place when it was a farmhouse and there was a little front porch.

I stopped before I opened the door and looked about a little. From where I stood I could look right down into the main street of the town, like being in a big city, like New York or Chicago, and looking down out of the fifteenth floor of an office building into the street.

The hillside was mighty steep and the road up had to wind and wind or no one could ever have come up out of the town to their plagued old fair at all.

It wasn't much of a town I saw—a main street with a lot of saloons and a few stores, one or two dinky moving-picture places, a few fords, hardly any women or girls in sight and a raft of men. I tried to think of the girl I had been dreaming about, as I walked around in the mud and darkness up at the fair ground, living in the place but I couldn't make it. It was like trying to think of Pick-it-boy getting himself worked up to the state I was in then, and going into the ugly dump I was going into. It couldn't be done.

All the same I knew the town wasn't all right there in sight. There must have been a good many of the kinds of houses Pennsylvania miners live in back in the hills, or around a turn in the valley in which the main street stood.

What I suppose is that, it being Saturday night and raining, the women and kids had all stayed at home and only the men were out, intending to get themselves liquored up. I've been in some other mining towns since and if I was a miner and had to live in one of them, or in one of the houses they live in with their women and kids, I'd get out and liquor myself up too.

So there I stood looking, and as sick as a dog inside myself, and as wet and cold as a rat in a sewer pipe. I could see the mass of dark figures moving about down below, and beyond the main street there was a river that made a sound you could hear distinctly, even up where I was, and over beyond the river were some railroad tracks with switch engines going up and down. I suppose they had something to do with the mines in which the men of the town worked. Anyway, as I stood watching and listening there was, now and then, a sound like thunder rolling down the sky, and I suppose that was a lot of coal, maybe a whole carload, being let down plunk into a coal car.

And then besides there was, on the side of a hill far

away, a long row of coke ovens. They had little doors, through which the light from the fire within leaked out and as they were set closely, side by side, they looked like the teeth of some big man-eating giant lying and waiting over there in the hills.

The sight of it all, even the sight of the kind of hell-holes men are satisfied to go on living in, gave me the fantods and the shivers right down in my liver, and on that night I guess I had in me a kind of contempt for all men, including myself, that I've never had so thoroughly since. Come right down to it, I suppose women aren't so much to blame as men. They aren't running the show.

Then I pushed open the door and went into the saloon. There were about a dozen men, miners I suppose, playing cards at tables in a little long dirty room, with a bar at one side of it, and with a big red-faced man with a mustache standing back of the bar.

The place smelled, as such places do where men hang around who have worked and sweated in their clothes and perhaps slept in them too, and have never had them washed but have just kept on wearing them. I guess you know what I mean if you've ever been in a city. You smell that smell in a city, in street cars on rainy nights when a lot of factory hands get on. I got pretty used to that smell when I was a tramp and pretty sick of it too.

And so I was in the place now, with a glass of whisky in my hand, and I thought all the miners were staring at me, which they weren't at all, but I thought they were and so I felt just the same as though they had been. And then I looked up and saw my own face in the old cracked looking-glass back of the bar. If the miners had been staring, or laughing at me, I wouldn't have wondered when I saw what I looked like.

It—I mean my own face—was white and pasty-looking, and for some reason, I can't tell exactly why, it wasn't my own face at all. It's a funny business I'm trying to tell you about and I know what you may be thinking of me as well as you do, so you needn't suppose I'm innocent or ashamed. I'm only wondering. I've thought about it a lot since and I can't make it out. I know I was never that way before that night and I know I've never been that way since. Maybe it was lonesomeness, just lonesomeness, gone on in me too long. I've often wondered if women generally are lonesomer than men.

The point is that the face I saw in the looking-glass back of that bar, when I looked up from my glass of whisky that evening, wasn't my own face at all but the face of a woman. It was a girl's face, that's what I mean. That's what it was. It was a girl's face, and a lonesome and scared girl too. She was just a kid at that.

When I saw that the glass of whisky came pretty near falling out of my hand but I gulped it down, put a dollar on the bar, and called for another. "I've got to be careful here — I'm up against something new," I said to myself. "If any of these men in here get on to me there's going to be trouble." When I had got the second drink in me I called for a third and I thought, "When I get this third drink down I'll get out of here and back up the hill to the fair ground before I make a fool of myself and begin to get drunk."

And then, while I was thinking and drinking my third glass of whisky, the men in the room began to laugh and of course I thought they were laughing at me. But they weren't. No one in the place had really paid any attention to me.

What they were laughing at was a man who had just come in at the door. I'd never seen such a fellow. He was a huge big man, with red hair, that stuck straight up like bristles out of his head, and he had a red-haired kid in his arms. The kid was just like himself, big, I mean, for his age, and with the same kind of stiff red hair.

He came and set the kid up on the bar, close beside me, and called for a glass of whisky for himself and all the men in the room began to shout and laugh at him and his kid. Only they didn't shout and laugh when he was looking, so he could tell which ones did it, but did all their shouting and laughing when his head was turned the other way. They kept calling him "cracked." "The crack is getting wider in the old tin pan," someone sang and then they all laughed.

I'm puzzled you see, just how to make you feel as I felt that night. I suppose, having undertaken to write this story, that's what I'm up against, trying to do that. I'm not claiming to be able to inform you or to do you any good. I'm just trying to make you understand some things about me, as I would like to understand some things about you, or anyone, if I had the chance. Anyway the whole blamed thing, the thing that went on I mean in that little saloon on that rainy Saturday night, wasn't like anything quite real. I've already told you how I had looked into the glass back of the bar and had seen there, not my own face but the face of a scared young girl. Well, the men, the miners, sitting at the tables in the half dark room, the red-faced bartender, the unholy looking big man who had come in and his queer-looking kid, now sitting on the bar — all of them were like characters in some play, not like real people at all.

There was myself, that wasn't myself—and I'm not any fairy. Anyone who has known me knows better than that.

And then there was the man who had come in. There was a feeling came out of him that wasn't like the feeling you get from a man at all. It was more like the feeling you get maybe from a horse, only his eyes weren't like a horse's eyes. Horses' eyes have a kind of calm something in them and his hadn't. If you've ever carried a lantern through a wood at night, going along a path, and then suddenly you felt something funny in the air and stopped, and there ahead of you somewhere were the eyes of some little animal, gleaming out at you from a dead wall of darkness—The eyes shine big and quiet but there is a point right in the centre of each, where there is something dancing and wavering. You aren't afraid the little animal will jump at you, you are afraid the little eyes will jump at you—that's what's the matter with you.

Only of course a horse, when you go into his stall at night, or a little animal you had disturbed in a wood that way, wouldn't be talking and the big man who had come in there with his kid was talking. He kept talking all the time, saying something under his breath, as they say, and I could only understand now and then a few words. It was his talking made him kind of terrible. His eyes said one thing and his lips another. They didn't seem to get together, as though they belonged to the same person.

For one thing the man was too big. There was about him an unnatural bigness. It was in his hands, his arms, his shoulders, his body, his head, a bigness like you might see in trees and bushes in a tropical country perhaps. I've never been in a tropical country but I've seen pictures. Only his eyes were small. In his big head they looked like the eyes of a bird. And I remember that his lips were thick, like negroes' lips.

He paid no attention to me or to the others in the room but kept on muttering to himself, or to the kid sitting on the bar—I couldn't tell to which.

First he had one drink and then, quick, another. I stood

staring at him and thinking — a jumble of thoughts, I suppose.

What I must have been thinking was something like this. "Well he's one of the kind you are always seeing about towns," I thought. I meant he was one of the cracked kind. In almost any small town you go to you will find one, and sometimes two or three cracked people, walking around. They go through the street, muttering to themselves and people generally are cruel to them. Their own folks make a bluff at being kind, but they aren't really, and the others in the town, men and boys, like to tease them. They send such a fellow, the mild silly kind, on some fool errand after a round square or a dozen post-holes or tie cards on his back saying "Kick me," or something like that, and then carry on and laugh as though they had done something funny.

And so there was this cracked one in that saloon and I could see the men in there wanted to have some fun putting up some kind of horseplay on him, but they didn't quite dare. He wasn't one of the mild kind, that was a cinch. I kept looking at the man and at his kid, and then up at that strange unreal reflection of myself in the cracked looking-glass back of the bar. "Rats, rats, digging in the ground—miners are rats, little jack-rabbit," I heard him say to his solemn-faced kid. I guess, after all, maybe he wasn't so cracked.

The kid sitting on the bar kept blinking at his father, like an owl caught out in the daylight, and now the father was having another glass of whisky. He drank six glasses, one right after the other, and it was cheap ten-cent stuff. He must have had cast-iron insides all right.

Of the men in the room there were two or three (maybe they were really more scared than the others so had to put up a bluff of bravery by showing off) who kept laughing and making funny cracks about the big man and his kid and there was one fellow was the worst of the bunch. I'll never forget that fellow because of his looks and what happened to him afterwards.

He was one of the showing-off kind all right, and he was the one that had started the song about the crack getting bigger in the old tin pan. He sang it two or three times, and then he grew bolder and got up and began walking up and down the room singing it over and over. He was a showy kind of man with a fancy vest, on which there were brown tobacco spots, and he wore glasses. Every time he made some crack he thought was funny, he winked at the others as though to say, "You see me. I'm not afraid of this big fellow," and then the others laughed.

The proprietor of the place must have known what was going on, and the danger in it, because he kept leaning over the bar and saying, "Shush, now quit it," to the showy-off man, but it didn't do any good. The fellow kept prancing like a turkey-cock and he put his hat on one side of his head and stopped right back of the big man and sang that song about the crack in the old tin pan. He was one of the kind you can't shush until they get their blocks knocked off, and it didn't take him long to come to it that time anyhow.

Because the big fellow just kept on muttering to his kid and drinking his whisky, as though he hadn't heard anything, and then suddenly he turned and his big hand flashed out and he grabbed, not the fellow who had been showing off, but me. With just a sweep of his arm he brought me up against his big body. Then he shoved me over with my breast jammed against the bar and looking right into his kid's face and he said, "Now you watch him, and if you let him fall I'll kill you," in just quiet ordinary tones as though he was saying "good morning" to some neighbor.

Then the kid leaned over and threw his arms around my head, and in spite of that I did manage to screw my head around enough to see what happened.

It was a sight I'll never forget. The big fellow had whirled around, and he had the showy-off man by the shoulder now, and the fellow's face was a sight. The big man must have had some reputation as a bad man in the town, even though he was cracked, for the man with the fancy vest had his mouth open now, and his hat had fallen off his head, and he was silent and scared. Once, when I was a tramp, I saw a kid killed by a train. The kid was walking on the rail and showing off before some other kids, by letting them see how close he could let an engine come to him before he got out of the way. And the engine was whistling and a woman, over on the porch of a house nearby, was jumping up and down and screaming, and the kid let the engine get nearer and nearer, wanting more and more to show off, and then he stumbled and fell. God, I'll never forget the look on his face, in just the second before he got hit and killed, and now, there in that saloon, was the same terrible look on another face.

I closed my eyes for a moment and was sick all through me and then, when I opened my eyes, the big man's fist was just coming down in the other man's face. The one blow knocked him cold and he fell down like a beast hit with an axe.

And then the most terrible thing of all happened. The big man had on heavy boots, and he raised one of them and brought it down on the other man's shoulder, as he lay white and groaning on the floor. I could hear the bones crunch and it made me so sick I could hardly stand up, but I had to stand up and hold on to that kid or I knew it would be my turn next.

Because the big fellow didn't seem excited or anything, but kept on muttering to himself as he had been doing when he was standing peacefully by the bar drinking his whisky, and now he had raised his foot again, and maybe this time he would bring it down in the other man's face and, "just eliminate his map for keeps," as sports and prize-fighters sometimes say. I trembled, like I was having a chill, but thank God at that moment the kid, who had his arms around me and one hand clinging to my nose, so that there were the marks of his finger-nails on it the next morning, at that moment the kid, thank God, began to howl, and his father didn't bother any more with the man on the floor but turned around, knocked me aside, and taking the kid in his arms tramped out of that place, muttering to himself as he had been doing ever since he came in.

I went out too but I didn't prance out with any dignity, I'll tell you that. I slunk out like a thief or a coward, which perhaps I am, partly anyhow.

And so there I was, outside there in the darkness, and it was as cold and wet and black and God-forsaken a night as any man ever saw. I was so sick at the thought of human beings that night I could have vomited to think of them at all. For a while I just stumbled along in the mud of the road, going up the hill, back to the fair ground, and then, almost before I knew where I was, I found myself in the stall with Pick-it-boy.

That was one of the best and sweetest feelings I've ever had in my whole life, being in that warm stall alone with that horse that night. I had told the other swipes that I would go up and down the row of stalls now and then and have an eye on the other horses, but I had altogether forgotten my promise now. I went and stood with my back against the side of the stall, thinking how mean and low and all balled-up and twisted-up human beings can become, and how the best of them are likely to get that way any time, just because they are human beings and not simple and clear in their minds, and inside themselves, as animals are, maybe.

Perhaps you know how a person feels at such a moment. There are things you think of, odd little things you had thought you had forgotten. Once, when you were a kid, you were with your father, and he was all dressed up, as for a funeral or Fourth of July, and was walking along a street holding your hand. And you were going past a railroad station, and there was a woman standing. She was a stranger in your town and was dressed as you had never seen a woman dressed before, and never thought you would see one, looking so nice. Long afterwards you knew that was because she had lovely taste in clothes, such as so few women have really, but then you thought she must be a queen. You had read about queens in fairy stories and the thoughts of them thrilled you. What lovely eyes the strange lady had and what beautiful rings she wore on her fingers.

Then your father came out, from being in the railroad station, maybe to set his watch by the station clock, and took you by the hand and he and the woman smiled at each other, in an embarrassed kind of way, and you kept looking longingly back at her, and when you were out of her hearing you asked your father if she really were a queen. And it may be that your father was one who wasn't so very hot on democracy and a free country and talked-up bunk about a free citizenry, and he said he hoped she was a queen, and maybe, for all he knew, she was.

Or maybe, when you get jammed up as I was that night, and can't get things clear about yourself or other people and why you are alive, or for that matter why anyone you can think about is alive, you think, not of people at all but of other things you have seen and felt — like walking along a road in the snow in the winter, perhaps out in Iowa, and hearing soft warm sounds in a barn close to the road, or of another time when you were on a hill and the sun was going down and the sky suddenly became a great soft-colored bowl, all glowing like a jewel-handled bowl, a great queen in some far away mighty kingdom might have put on a vast table out under the tree, once a year, when she invited all her loyal and loving subjects to come and dine with her.

I can't, of course, figure out what you try to think about when you are as desolate as I was that night. Maybe you are like me and inclined to think of women, and maybe you are like a man I met once, on the road, who told me that when he was up against it he never thought of anything but grub and a big nice clean warm bed to sleep in. "I don't care about anything else and I don't ever let myself think of anything else," he said. "If I was like you and went to thinking about women sometime I'd find myself hooked up to some skirt, and she'd have the old double cross on me, and the rest of my life maybe I'd be working in some factory for her and her kids."

As I say, there I was anyway, up there alone with that horse in that warm stall in that dark lonesome fair ground and I had that feeling about being sick at the thought of human beings and what they could be like.

Well, suddenly I got again the queer feeling I'd had about him once or twice before, I mean the feeling about our understanding each other in some way I can't explain.

So having it again I went over to where he stood and began running my hands all over his body, just because I loved the feel of him and as sometimes, to tell the plain

THE MAN WHO BECAME A WOMAN

truth, I've felt about touching with my hands the body of a woman I've seen and who I thought was lovely too. I ran my hands over his head and neck and then down over his hard firm round body and then over his flanks and down his legs. His flanks quivered a little I remember and once he turned his head and stuck his cold nose down along my neck and nipped my shoulder a little, in a soft playful way. It hurt a little but I didn't care.

So then I crawled up through a hole into the loft above thinking that night was over anyway and glad of it, but it wasn't, not by a long sight.

As my clothes were all soaking wet and as we race track swipes didn't own any such things as night-gowns or pajamas I had to go to bed naked, of course.

But we had plenty of horse blankets and so I tucked myself in between a pile of them and tried not to think any more that night. The being with Pick-it-boy and having him close right under me that way made me feel a little better.

Then I was sound asleep and dreaming and—bang like being hit with a club by someone who has sneaked up behind you — I got another wallop.

What I suppose is that, being upset the way I was, I had forgotten to bolt the door to Pick-it-boy's stall down below and two negro men had come in there, thinking they were in their own place, and had climbed through the hole where I was. They were half lit up but not what you might call dead drunk, and I suppose they were up against something a couple of white swipes, who had some money in their pockets, wouldn't have been up against.

What I mean is that a couple of white swipes, having liquored themselves up and being down there in the town on a bat, if they wanted a woman or a couple of women would have been able to find them. There is always a few women of that kind can be found around any town I've ever seen or heard of, and of course a bar tender would have given them the tip where to go.

But a negro, up there in that country, where there aren't any, or anyway mighty few negro women, wouldn't know what to do when he felt that way and would be up against it.

It's so always. Burt and several other negroes I've known pretty well have talked to me about it, lots of times. You take now a young negro man—not a race track swipe or a tramp or any other low-down kind of fellow—but, let us say, one who has been to college, and has behaved himself and tried to be a good man, the best he could, and be clean, as they say. He isn't any better off, is he? If he has made himself some money and wants to go sit in a swell restaurant, or go to hear some good music, or see a good play at the theatre, he gets what we used to call on the tracks, "the messy end of the dung fork," doesn't he?

And even in such a low-down place as what people call a "bad house" it's the same way. The white swipes and others can go into a place where they have negro women fast enough, and they do it too, but you let a negro swipe try it the other way around and see how he comes out.

You see, I can think this whole thing out fairly now, sitting here in my own house and writing, and with my wife Jessie in the kitchen making a pie or something, and I can show just how the two negro men who came into that loft, where I was asleep, were justified in what they did, and I can preach about how the negroes are up against it in this country, like a daisy, but I tell you what, I didn't think things out that way that night.

For, you understand, what they thought, they being half liquored-up, and when one of them had jerked the blankets off me, was that I was a woman. One of them carried a lantern but it was smoky and dirty and didn't give out much light. So they must have figured it out—my body being pretty white and slender then, like a young girl's body I suppose—that some kind of girls around a town that will come with a swipe to a race track on a rainy night aren't very fancy females but you'll find that kind in the towns all right. I've seen many a one in my day.

And so, I figure, these two big buck niggers, being piped that way, just made up their minds they would snatch me away from the white swipe who had brought me out there, and who had left me lying carelessly around.

"Jes' you lie still honey. We ain't gwine hurt you none," one of them said, with a little chuckling laugh that had something in it besides a laugh, too. It was the kind of laugh that gives you the shivers.

The devil of it was I couldn't say anything, not even a word. Why I couldn't yell out and say "What the hell," and just kid them a little and shoo them out of there I don't know, but I couldn't. I tried and tried so that my throat hurt but I didn't say a word. I just lay there staring at them.

It was a mixed-up night. I've never gone through another night like it.

Was I scared? Lord Almighty, I'll tell you what, I was scared.

Because the two big black faces were leaning right over me now, and I could feel their liquored-up breaths on my cheeks, and their eyes were shining in the dim light from that smoky lantern, and right in the centre of their eyes was that dancing flickering light I've told you about your seeing in the eyes of wild animals, when you were carrying a lantern through the woods at night.

It was a puzzler! All my life, you see—me never having had any sisters, and at that time never having had a sweetheart either—I had been dreaming and thinking about women, and I suppose I'd always been dreaming about a pure innocent one, for myself, made for me by God, maybe. Men are that way. No matter how big they talk about "let the women go hang," they've always got that notion tucked away inside themselves, somewhere. It's a kind of chesty man's notion, I suppose, but they've got it and the kind of up-and-coming women we have nowadays who are always saying, "I'm as good as a man and will do what the men do," are on the wrong trail if they really ever want to, what you might say "hog-tie" a fellow of their own.

So I had invented a kind of princess, with black hair and a slender willowy body to dream about. And I thought of her as being shy and afraid to ever tell anything she really felt to anyone but just me. I suppose I fancied that if I ever found such a woman in the flesh I would be the strong sure one and she the timid shrinking one.

And now I was that woman, or something like her, myself.

I gave a kind of wriggle, like a fish, you have just taken off the hook. What I did next wasn't a thought-out thing. I was caught and I squirmed, that's all.

The two niggers both jumped at me but somehow—the lantern having been kicked over and having gone out the first move they made—well in some way, when they both lunged at me they missed.

As good luck would have it my feet found the hole, where you put hay down to the horse in the stall below, and through which we crawled up when it was time to go to bed in our blankets up in the hay, and down I slid, not bothering to try to find the ladder with my feet but just letting myself go.

In less than a second I was out of doors in the dark and the rain and the two blacks were down the hole and out the door of the stall after me.

How long or how far they really followed me I suppose I'll never know. It was black dark and raining hard now and a roaring wind had begun to blow. Of course, my body being white, it must have made some kind of faint streak in the darkness as I ran, and anyway I thought they could see me and I knew I couldn't see them and that made my terror ten times worse. Every minute I thought they would grab me.

You know how it is when a person is all upset and full of terror as I was. I suppose maybe the two niggers followed me for a while, running across the muddy race track and into the grove of trees that grew in the oval inside the track, but likely enough, after just a few minutes, they gave up the chase and went back, found their own place and went to sleep. They were liquored-up, as I've said, and maybe partly funning too.

But I didn't know that, if they were. As I ran I kept hearing sounds, sounds made by the rain coming down through the dead old leaves left on the trees and by the wind blowing, and it may be that the sound that scared me most of all was my own bare feet stepping on a dead branch and breaking it or something like that.

There was something strange and scary, a steady sound, like a heavy man running and breathing hard, right at my shoulder. It may have been my own breath, coming quick and fast. And I thought I heard that chuckling laugh I'd heard up in the loft, the laugh that sent the shivers right down through me. Of course every tree I came close to looked like a man standing there, ready to grab me, and I kept dodging and going — bang — into other trees. My shoulders kept knocking against trees in that way and the skin was all knocked off, and every time it happened I thought a big black hand had come down and clutched at me and was tearing my flesh.

How long it went on I don't know, maybe an hour, maybe five minutes. But anyway the darkness didn't let up, and the terror didn't let up, and I couldn't, to save my life, scream or make any sound.

Just why I couldn't I don't know. Could it be because at the time I was a woman, while at the same time I wasn't a woman? It may be that I was too ashamed of having turned into a girl and being afraid of a man to make any sound. I don't know about that. It's over my head.

But anyway I couldn't make a sound. I tried and tried and my throat hurt from trying and no sound came.

And then, after a long time, or what seemed like a long time, I got out from among the trees inside the track and was on the track itself again. I thought the two black men were still after me, you understand, and I ran like a madman.

Of course, running along the track that way, it must have been up the back stretch, I came after a time to where the old slaughter-house stood, in that field, beside the track. I knew it by its ungodly smell, scared as I was. Then, in some way, I managed to get over the high old fairground fence and was in the field, where the slaughter-house was.

All the time I was trying to yell or scream, or be sensible and tell those two black men that I was a man and not a woman, but I couldn't make it. And then I heard a sound like a board cracking or breaking in the fence and thought they were still after me.

So I kept on running like a crazy man, in the field, and

just then I stumbled and fell over something. I've told you how the old slaughter-house field was filled with bones, that had been lying there a long time and had all been washed white. There were heads of sheep and cows and all kinds of things.

And when I fell and pitched forward I fell right into the midst of something, still and cold and white.

It was probably the skeleton of a horse lying there. In small towns like that, they take an old worn-out horse, that has died, and haul him off to some field outside of town and skin him for the hide, that they can sell for a dollar or two. It doesn't make any difference what the horse has been, that's the way he usually ends up. Maybe even Pick-it-boy, or O My Man, or a lot of other good fast ones I've seen and known have ended that way by this time.

And so I think it was the bones of a horse lying there and he must have been lying on his back. The birds and wild animals had picked all his flesh away and the rain had washed his bones clean.

Anyway I fell and pitched forward and my side got cut pretty deep and my hands clutched at something. I had fallen right in between the ribs of the horse and they seemed to wrap themselves around me close. And my hands, clutching upwards, had got hold of the cheeks of that dead horse and the bones of his cheeks were cold as ice with the rain washing over them. White bones wrapped around me and white bones in my hands.

There was a new terror now that seemed to go down to the very bottom of me, to the bottom of the inside of me, I mean. It shook me like I have seen a rat in a barn shaken by a dog. It was a terror like a big wave that hits you when you are walking on a seashore, maybe. You see it coming and you try to run and get away but when you start to run inshore there is a stone cliff you can't climb. So the wave comes high as a mountain, and there it is, right in front of you and nothing in all this world can stop it. And now it had knocked you down and rolled and tumbled you over and over and washed you clean, clean, but dead maybe.

And that's the way I felt—I seemed to myself dead with blind terror. It was a feeling like the finger of God running down your back and burning you clean, I mean.

It burned all that silly nonsense about being a girl right out of me.

I screamed at last and the spell that was on me was broken. I'll bet the scream I let out of me could have been heard a mile and a half.

Right away I felt better and crawled out from among the pile of bones, and then I stood on my own feet again and I wasn't a woman, or a young girl any more but a man and my own self, and as far as I know I've been that way ever since. Even the black night seemed warm and alive now, like a mother might be to a kid in the dark.

Only I couldn't go back to the race track because I was blubbering and crying and was ashamed of myself and of what a fool I had made of myself. Someone might see me and I couldn't stand that, not at that moment.

So I went across the field, walking now, not running like a crazy man, and pretty soon I came to a fence and crawled over and got into another field, in which there was a straw stack, I just happened to find in the pitch darkness.

The straw stack had been there a long time and some sheep had nibbled away at it until they had made a pretty deep hole, like a cave, in the side of it. I found the hole and crawled in and there were some sheep in there, about a dozen of them.

When I came in, creeping on my hands and knees, they

didn't make much fuss, just stirred around a little and then settled down.

So I settled down amongst them too. They were warm and gentle and kind, like Pick-it-boy, and being in there with them made me feel better than I would have felt being with any human person I knew at that time.

So I settled down and slept after a while, and when I woke up it was daylight and not very cold and the rain was over. The clouds were breaking away from the sky now and maybe there would be a fair the next week but if there was I knew I wouldn't be there to see it.

Because what I expected to happen did happen. I had to go back across the fields and the fairground to the place where my clothes were, right in the broad daylight, and me stark naked, and of course I knew someone would be up and would raise a shout and every swipe and every driver would stick his head out and would whoop with laughter.

And there would be a thousand questions asked, and I would be too mad and too ashamed to answer, and would perhaps begin to blubber, and that would make me more ashamed than ever.

It all turned out just as I expected, except that when the noise and the shouts of laughter were going it the loudest, Burt came out of the stall where O My Man was kept, and when he saw me he didn't know what was the matter but he knew something was up that wasn't on the square and for which I wasn't to blame.

So he got so all-fired mad he couldn't speak for a minute, and then he grabbed a pitchfork and began prancing up and down before the other stalls, giving that gang of swipes and drivers such a royal old dressing-down as you never heard. You should have heard him sling language. It was grand to hear.

And while he was doing it I sneaked up into the loft, blubbering because I was so pleased and happy to hear him swear that way, and I got my wet clothes on quick and got down, and gave Pick-it-boy a good-bye kiss on the cheek and lit out.

The last I saw of all that part of my life was Burt, still going it, and yelling out for the man who had put up a trick on me to come out and get what was coming to him. He had the pitchfork in his hand and was swinging it around, and every now and then he would make a kind of lunge at a tree or something, he was so mad through, and there was no one else in sight at all. And Burt didn't even see me cutting out along the fence through a gate and down the hill and out of the race-horse and tramp life for the rest of my days.

Death in the Woods

S he was an old woman and lived on a farm near the town in which I lived. All country and small-town people have seen such old women, but no one knows much about them. Such an old woman comes into town driving an old worn-out horse or she comes afoot carrying a basket. She may own a few hens and have eggs to sell. She brings them in a basket and takes them to a grocer. There she trades them in. She gets some salt pork and some beans. Then she gets a pound or two of sugar and some flour.

Afterwards she goes to the butcher's and asks for some dog-meat. She may spend ten or fifteen cents, but when she does she asks for something. Formerly the butchers gave liver to any one who wanted to carry it away. In our family we were always having it. Once one of my brothers got a whole cow's liver at the slaughter-house near the fairgrounds in our town. We had it until we were sick of it. It never cost a cent. I have hated the thought of it ever since.

The old farm woman got some liver and a soupbone. She never visited with any one, and as soon as she got what she wanted she lit out for home. It made quite a load for such an old body. No one gave her a lift. People drive right down a road and never notice an old woman like that.

There was such an old woman who used to come into town past our house one Summer and Fall when I was a young boy and was sick with what was called inflammatory rheumatism. She went home later carrying a heavy pack on her back. Two or three large gaunt-looking dogs followed at her heels.

The old woman was nothing special. She was one of the nameless ones that hardly any one knows, but she got into my thoughts. I have just suddenly now, after all these years, remembered her and what happened. It is a story. Her name was Grimes, and she lived with her husband and son in a small unpainted house on the bank of a small creek four miles from town.

The husband and son were a tough lot. Although the son was but twenty-one, he had already served a term in jail. It was whispered about that the woman's husband stole horses and ran them off to some other county. Now and then, when a horse turned up missing, the man had also disappeared. No one ever caught him. Once, when I was loafing at Tom Whitehead's livery-barn, the man came there and sat on the bench in front. Two or three other men were there, but no one spoke to him. He sat for a few minutes and then got up and went away. When he was leaving he turned around and stared at the men. There was a look of defiance in his eyes. "Well, I have tried to be friendly. You don't want to talk to me. It has been so wherever I have gone in this town. If, some day, one of your fine horses turns up missing, well, then what?" He did not say anything actually. "I'd like to bust one of you on the jaw," was about what his eyes said. I remember how the look in his eyes made me shiver.

The old man belonged to a family that had had money

once. His name was Jake Grimes. It all comes back clearly
now. His father, John Grimes, had owned a sawmill when
the country was new, and had made money. Then he got
to drinking and running after women. When he died
there wasn't much left.

Jake blew in the rest. Pretty soon there wasn't any more
lumber to cut and his land was nearly all gone.

He got his wife off a German farmer, for whom he went
to work one June day in the wheat harvest. She was a
young thing then and scared to death. You see, the
farmer was up to something with the girl — she was, I
think, a bound girl and his wife had her suspicions. She
took it out on the girl when the man wasn't around. Then,
when the wife had to go off to town for supplies, the
farmer got after her. She told young Jake that nothing
really ever happened, but he didn't know whether to
believe it or not.

He got her pretty easy himself, the first time he was out
with her. He wouldn't have married her if the German
farmer hadn't tried to tell him where to get off. He got
her to go riding with him in his buggy one night when he
was threshing on the place, and then he came for her the
next Sunday night.

She managed to get out of the house without her
employer's seeing, but when she was getting into the
buggy he showed up. It was almost dark, and he just
popped up suddenly at the horse's head. He grabbed the
horse by the bridle and Jake got out his buggy-whip.

They had it out all right! The German was a tough one.
Maybe he didn't care whether his wife knew or not. Jake
hit him over the face and shoulders with the buggy-whip,
but the horse got to acting up and he had to get out.

Then the two men went for it. The girl didn't see it.
The horse started to run away and went nearly a mile

down the road before the girl got him stopped. Then she managed to tie him to a tree beside the road. (I wonder how I know all this. It must have stuck in my mind from small-town tales when I was a boy.) Jake found her there after he got through with the German. She was huddled up in the buggy seat, crying, scared to death. She told Jake a lot of stuff, how the German had tried to get her, how he chased her once into the barn, how another time, when they happened to be alone in the house together, he tore her dress open clear down the front. The German, she said, might have got her that time if he hadn't heard his old woman drive in at the gate. She had been off to town for supplies. Well, she would be putting the horse in the barn. The German managed to sneak off to the fields without his wife seeing. He told the girl he would kill her if she told. What could she do? She told a lie about ripping her dress in the barn when she was feeding the stock. I remember now that she was a bound girl and did not know where her father and mother were. Maybe she did not have any father. You know what I mean.

Such bound children were often enough cruelly treated. They were children who had no parents, slaves really. There were very few orphan homes then. They were legally bound into some home. It was a matter of pure luck how it came out.

II

SHE married Jake and had a son and daughter, but the daughter died.

Then she settled down to feed stock. That was her job. At the German's place she had cooked the food for the German and his wife. The wife was a strong woman with big hips and worked most of the time in the fields with her husband. She fed them and fed the cows in the barn, fed the pigs, the horses and the chickens. Every moment of every day, as a young girl, was spent feeding something.

Then she married Jake Grimes and he had to be fed. She was a slight thing, and when she had been married for three or four years, and after the two children were born, her slender shoulders became stooped.

Jake always had a lot of big dogs around the house, that stood near the unused sawmill near the creek. He was always trading horses when he wasn't stealing something and had a lot of poor bony ones about. Also he kept three or four pigs and a cow. They were all pastured in the few acres left of the Grimes place and Jake did little enough work.

He went into debt for a threshing outfit and ran it for several years, but it did not pay. People did not trust him. They were afraid he would steal the grain at night. He had to go a long way off to get work and it cost too much to get there. In the Winter he hunted and cut a little firewood, to be sold in some nearby town. When the son grew up he was just like the father. They got drunk together. If there wasn't anything to eat in the house when they came home the old man gave his old woman a cut over the head. She had a few chickens of her own and had to kill one of them in a hurry. When they were all killed she wouldn't have any eggs to sell when she went to town, and then what would she do?

She had to scheme all her life about getting things fed, getting the pigs fed so they would grow fat and could be butchered in the Fall. When they were butchered her husband took most of the meat off to town and sold it. If he did not do it first the boy did. They fought sometimes and when they fought the old woman stood aside trembling.

She had got the habit of silence anyway — that was fixed. Sometimes, when she began to look old — she wasn't forty yet — and when the husband and son were both off, trading horses or drinking or hunting or stealing, she went around the house and the barnyard muttering to herself.

How was she going to get everything fed? — that was her problem. The dogs had to be fed. There wasn't enough hay in the barn for the horses and the cow. If she didn't feed the chickens how could they lay eggs? Without eggs to sell how could she get things in town, things she had to have to keep the life of the farm going? Thank heaven, she did not have to feed her husband — in a certain way. That hadn't lasted long after their marriage and after the babies came. Where he went on his long trips she did not know. Sometimes he was gone from home for weeks, and after the boy grew up they went off together.

They left everything at home for her to manage and she had no money. She knew no one. No one ever talked to her in town. When it was Winter she had to gather sticks of wood for her fire, had to try to keep the stock fed with very little grain.

The stock in the barn cried to her hungrily, the dogs followed her about. In the Winter the hens laid few enough eggs. They huddled in the corners of the barn and she kept watching them. If a hen lays an egg in the barn in the Winter and you do not find it, it freezes and breaks.

One day in Winter the old woman went off to town with a few eggs and the dogs followed her. She did not get started until nearly three o'clock and the snow was heavy. She hadn't been feeling very well for several days and so she went muttering along, scantily clad, her shoulders stooped. She had an old grain bag in which she carried her eggs, tucked away down in the bottom. There weren't many of them, but in Winter the price of eggs is up. She would get a little meat in exchange for the eggs, some salt pork, a little sugar, and some coffee perhaps. It might be the butcher would give her a piece of liver.

When she had got to town and was trading in her eggs the dogs lay by the door outside. She did pretty well, got the things she needed, more than she had hoped. Then she went to the butcher and he gave her some liver and some dog-meat.

It was the first time any one had spoken to her in a friendly way for a long time. The butcher was alone in his shop when she came in and was annoyed by the thought of such a sick-looking old woman out on such a day. It was bitter cold and the snow, that had let up during the afternoon, was falling again. The butcher said something about her husband and her son, swore at them, and the old woman stared at him, a look of mild surprise in her eyes as he talked. He said that if either the husband or the son were going to get any of the liver or the heavy bones with scraps of meat hanging to them that he had put into the grain bag, he'd see him starve first.

Starve, eh? Well, things had to be fed. Men had to be fed, and the horses that weren't any good but maybe could be traded off, and the poor thin cow that hadn't given any milk for three months.

Horses, cows, pigs, dogs, men.

III

THE old woman had to get back before darkness came if she could. The dogs followed at her heels, sniffing at the heavy grain bag she had fastened on her back. When she got to the edge of town she stopped by a fence and tied the bag on her back with a piece of rope she had carried in her dress-pocket for just that purpose. That was an easier way to carry it. Her arms ached. It was hard when she had to crawl over fences and once she fell over and landed in the snow. The dogs went frisking about. She had to struggle to get to her feet again, but she made it. The point of climbing over the fences was that there was a short cut over a hill and through a woods. She might have gone around by the road, but it was a mile farther that way. She was afraid she couldn't make it. And then, besides, the stock had to be fed. There was a little hay left and a little corn. Perhaps her husband and son would bring some home when they came. They had driven off in the only buggy the Grimes family had, a rickety thing, a rickety horse hitched to the buggy, two other rickety horses led by halters. They were going to trade horses, get a little money if they could. They might come home drunk. It would be well to have something in the house when they came back.

The son had an affair on with a woman at the county seat, fifteen miles away. She was a rough enough woman, a tough one. Once, in the Summer, the son had brought her to the house. Both she and the son had been drinking. Jake Grimes was away and the son and his woman ordered the old woman about like a servant. She didn't mind much; she was used to it. Whatever happened she never said anything. That was her way of getting along. She had managed that way when she was a young girl at the German's and ever since she had married Jake. That time her son brought his woman to the house they stayed all night, sleeping together just as though they were married. It hadn't shocked the old woman, not much. She had got past being shocked early in life.

With the pack on her back she went painfully along

across an open field, wading in the deep snow, and got into the woods.

There was a path, but it was hard to follow. Just beyond the top of the hill, where the woods was thickest, there was a small clearing. Had some one once thought of building a house there? The clearing was as large as a building lot in town, large enough for a house and a garden. The path ran along the side of the clearing, and when she got there the old woman sat down to rest at the foot of a tree.

It was a foolish thing to do. When she got herself placed, the pack against the tree's trunk, it was nice, but what about getting up again? She worried about that for a moment and then quietly closed here eyes.

She must have slept for a time. When you are about so cold you can't get any colder. The afternoon grew a little warmer and the snow came thicker than ever. Then after a time the weather cleared. The moon even came out.

There were four Grimes dogs that had followed Mrs. Grimes into town, all tall gaunt fellows. Such men as Jake Grimes and his son always keep just such dogs. They kick and abuse them, but they stay. The Grimes dogs, in order to keep from starving, had to do a lot of foraging for themselves, and they had been at it while the old woman slept with her back to the tree at the side of the clearing. They had been chasing rabbits in the woods and in adjoining fields and in their ranging had picked up three other farm dogs.

After a time all the dogs came back to the clearing. They were excited about something. Such nights, cold and clear and with a moon, do things to dogs. It may be that some old instinct, come down from the time when they were wolves and ranged the woods in packs on Winter nights, comes back into them.

The dogs in the clearing, before the old woman, had caught two or three rabbits and their immediate hunger had been satisfied. They began to play, running in circles in the clearing. Round and round they ran, each dog's nose at the tail of the next dog. In the clearing, under the snow-laden trees and under the wintry moon they made a strange picture, running thus silently, in a circle their running had beaten in the soft snow. The dogs made no sound. They ran around and around in the circle.

It may have been that the old woman saw them doing that before she died. She may have awakened once or twice and looked at the strange sight with dim old eyes.

She wouldn't be very cold now, just drowsy. Life hangs on a long time. Perhaps the old woman was out of her head. She may have dreamed of her girlhood, at the German's, and before that, when she was a child and before her mother lit out and left her.

Her dreams couldn't have been very pleasant. Not many pleasant things had happened to her. Now and then one of the Grimes dogs left the running circle and came to stand before her. The dog thrust his face close to her face. His red tongue was hanging out.

The running of the dogs may have been a kind of death ceremony. It may have been that the primitive instinct of the wolf, having been aroused in the dogs by the night and the running, made them somehow afraid.

"Now we are no longer wolves. We are dogs, the servants of men. Keep alive, man! When man dies we become wolves again."

When one of the dogs came to where the old woman sat with her back against the tree and thrust his nose close to her face he seemed satisfied and went back to run with the pack. All the Grimes dogs did it at some time during the evening, before she died. I knew all about it after-

ward, when I grew to be a man, because once in a woods
in Illinois, on another Winter night, I saw a pack of dogs
act just like that. The dogs were waiting for me to die as
they had waited for the old woman that night when I was
a child, but when it happened to me I was a young man
and had no intention whatever of dying.

The old woman died softly and quietly. When she was
dead and when one of the Grimes dogs had come to her
and had found her dead all the dogs stopped running.

They gathered about her.

Well, she was dead now. She had fed the Grimes dogs
when she was alive, what about now?

There was the pack on her back, the grain bag containing the piece of salt pork, the liver the butcher had given
her, the dog-meat, the soup bones. The butcher in town,
having been suddenly overcome with a feeling of pity,
had loaded her grain bag heavily. It had been a big haul
for the old woman.

It was a big haul for the dogs now.

IV

ONE of the Grimes dogs sprang suddenly out from
among the others and began worrying the pack on the
old woman's back. Had the dogs really been wolves that
one would have been the leader of the pack. What he did,
all the others did.

All of them sank their teeth into the grain bag the old
woman had fastened with ropes to her back.

They dragged the old woman's body out into the open
clearing. The worn-out dress was quickly torn from her
shoulders. When she was found, a day or two later, the
dress had been torn from her body clear to the hips, but
the dogs had not touched her body. They had got the
meat out of the grain bag, that was all. Her body was

frozen stiff when it was found, and the shoulders were so narrow and the body so slight that in death it looked like the body of some charming young girl.

Such things happened in towns of the Middle West, on farms near town, when I was a boy. A hunter out after rabbits found the old woman's body and did not touch it. Something, the beaten round path in the little snow-covered clearing, the silence of the place, the place where the dogs had worried the body trying to pull the grain bag away or tear it open — something startled the man and he hurried off to town.

I was in Main Street with one of my brothers who was town newsboy and who was taking the afternoon papers to the stores. It was almost night.

The hunter came into a grocery and told his story. Then he went to a hardware-shop and into a drugstore. Men began to gather on the sidewalks. Then they started out along the road to the place in the woods.

My brother should have gone on about his business of distributing papers but he didn't. Every one was going to the woods. The undertaker went and the town marshal. Several men got on a dray and rode out to where the path left the road and went into the woods, but the horses weren't very sharply shod and slid about on the slippery roads. They made no better time than those of us who walked.

The town marshal was a large man whose leg had been injured in the Civil War. He carried a heavy cane and limped rapidly along the road. My brother and I followed at his heels, and as we went other men and boys joined the crowd.

It had grown dark by the time we got to where the old woman had left the road but the moon had come out. The marshal was thinking there might have been a murder. He kept asking the hunter questions. The hunter went along with his gun across his shoulders, a dog following at his heels. It isn't often a rabbit hunter has a chance to be so conspicuous. He was taking full advantage of it, leading the procession with the town marshal. "I didn't see any wounds. She was a beautiful young girl. Her face was buried in the snow. No, I didn't know her." As a matter of fact, the hunter had not looked closely at the body. He had been frightened. She might have been murdered and some one might spring out from behind a tree and murder him. In a woods, in the late afternoon, when the trees are all bare and there is white snow on the ground, when all is silent, something creepy steals over the mind and body. If something strange or uncanny has happened in the neighborhood all you think about is getting away from there as fast as you can.

The crowd of men and boys had got to where the old woman had crossed the field and went, following the marshal and the hunter, up the slight incline and into the woods.

My brother and I were silent. He had his bundle of papers in a bag slung across his shoulder. When he got back to town he would have to go on distributing his papers before he went home to supper. If I went along, as he had no doubt already determined I should, we would both be late. Either mother or our older sister would have to warm our supper.

Well, we would have something to tell. A boy did not get such a chance very often. It was lucky we just happened to go into the grocery when the hunter came in. The hunter was a country fellow. Neither of us had ever seen him before.

Now the crowd of men and boys had got to the clearing. Darkness comes quickly on such Winter nights, but the full moon made everything clear. My brother and I stood near the tree, beneath which the old woman had died.

She did not look old, lying there in that light, frozen and still. One of the men turned her over in the snow and I saw everything. My body trembled with some strange mystical feeling and so did my brother's. It might have been the cold.

Neither of us had ever seen a woman's body before. It may have been the snow, clinging to the frozen flesh, that made it look so white and lovely, so like marble. No woman had come with the party from town; but one of the men, he was the town blacksmith, took off his overcoat and spread it over her. Then he gathered her into his arms and started off to town, all the others following silently. At that time no one knew who she was.

V

I had seen everything, had seen the oval in the snow, like a miniature race-track, where the dogs had run, had seen how the men were mystified, had seen the white bare young-looking shoulders, had heard the whispered comments of the men.

The men were simply mystified. They took the body to the undertaker's, and when the blacksmith, the hunter, the marshal and several others had got inside they closed the door. If father had been there perhaps he could have got in, but we boys couldn't.

I went with my brother to distribute the rest of his papers and when we got home it was my brother who told the story.

I kept silent and went to bed early. It may have been I was not satisfied with the way he told it.

Later, in the town, I must have heard other fragments

of the old woman's story. She was recognized the next day and there was an investigation.

The husband and son were found somewhere and brought to town and there was an attempt to connect them with the woman's death, but it did not work. They had perfect enough alibis.

However, the town was against them. They had to get out. Where they went I never heard.

I remember only the picture there in the forest, the men standing about, the naked girlish-looking figure, face down in the snow, the tracks made by the running dogs and the clear cold Winter sky above. White fragments of clouds were drifting across the sky. They went racing across the little open space among the trees.

The scene in the forest had become for me, without my knowing it, the foundation for the real story I am now trying to tell. The fragments, you see, had to be picked up slowly, long afterwards.

Things happened. When I was a young man I worked on the farm of a German. The hired-girl was afraid of her employer. The farmer's wife hated her.

I saw things at that place. Once later, I had a half-uncanny, mystical adventure with dogs in an Illinois forest on a clear, moon-lit Winter night. When I was a schoolboy, and on a Summer day, I went with a boy friend out along a creek some miles from town and came to the house where the old woman had lived. No one had lived in the house since her death. The doors were broken from the hinges; the window lights were all broken. As the boy and I stood in the road outside, two dogs, just roving farm dogs no doubt, came running around the corner of the house. The dogs were tall, gaunt fellows and came down to the fence and glared through at us, standing in the road.

The whole thing, the story of the old woman's death, was to me as I grew older like music heard from far off. The notes had to be picked up slowly one at a time. Something had to be understood.

The woman who died was one destined to feed animal life. Anyway, that is all she ever did. She was feeding animal life before she was born, as a child, as a young woman working on the farm of the German, after she married, when she grew old and when she died. She fed animal life in cows, in chickens, in pigs, in horses, in dogs, in men. Her daughter had died in childhood and with her one son she had no articulate relations. On the night when she died she was hurrying homeward, bearing on her body food for animal life.

She died in the clearing in the woods and even after her death continued feeding animal life.

You see it is likely that, when my brother told the story, that night when we got home and my mother and sister sat listening, I did not think he got the point. He was too young and so was I. A thing so complete has its own beauty.

I shall not try to emphasize the point. I am only explaining why I was dissatisfied then and have been ever since. I speak of that only that you may understand why I have been impelled to try to tell the simple story over again.

Brother Death

There were the two oak stumps, knee high to a not-too-tall man and cut quite squarely across. They became to the two children objects of wonder. They had seen the two trees cut but had run away just as the trees fell. They hadn't thought of the two stumps, to be left standing there; hadn't even looked at them. Afterwards Ted said to his sister Mary, speaking of the stumps: "I wonder if they bled, like legs, when a surgeon cuts a man's leg off." He had been hearing war stories. A man came to the farm one day to visit one of the farm-hands, a man who had been in the World War and had lost an arm. He stood in one of the barns talking. When Ted said that Mary spoke up at once. She hadn't been lucky enough to be at the barn when the one-armed man was there talking, and was jealous. "Why not a woman or a girl's leg?" she said, but Ted said the idea was silly. "Women and girls don't get their legs and arms cut off," he declared. "Why not? I'd just like to know why not?" Mary kept saying.

It would have been something if they had stayed, that day the trees were cut. "We might have gone and touched the places," Ted said. He meant the stumps. Would they have been warm? Would they have bled? They did go and touch the places afterwards, but it was a cold day and the stumps were cold. Ted stuck to his point that only men's arms and legs were cut off, but Mary thought of automobile accidents. "You can't think just about wars. There might be an automobile accident," she declared, but Ted wouldn't be convinced.

They were both children, but something had made them both in an odd way old. Mary was fourteen and Ted eleven, but Ted wasn't strong and that rather evened things up. They were the children of a well-to-do Virginia farmer named John Grey in the Blue Ridge country in Southwestern Virginia. There was a wide valley called the "Rich Valley," with a railroad and a small river running through it and high mountains in sight, to the north and south. Ted had some kind of heart disease, a lesion, something of the sort, the result of a severe attack of diptheria when he was a child of eight. He was thin and not strong but curiously alive. The doctor said he might die at any moment, might just drop down dead. The fact had drawn him peculiarly close to his sister Mary. It had awakened a strong and determined maternalism in her.

The whole family, the neighbors, on neighboring farms in the valley, and even the other children at the schoolhouse where they went to school recognized something as existing between the two children. "Look at them going along there," people said. "They do seem to have good times together, but they are so serious. For such young children they are too serious. Still, I suppose, under the circumstances, it's natural." Of course, everyone knew about Ted. It had done something to Mary. At fourteen she was both a child and a grown woman. The woman side of her kept popping out at unexpected moments.

People wondered why Louise Aspinwahl had married John Grey, but when they were wondering they smiled.

The Aspinwahl girls were all well educated, had all been away to college, but Louise wasn't so pretty. She got nicer after marriage, suddenly almost beautiful. The Aspinwahls were, as every one knew, naturally sensitive, really first class but the men couldn't hang onto land and the Greys could. In all that section of Virginia, people gave John Grey credit for being what he was. They respected him. "He's on the level," they said, "as honest as a horse. He has cattle sense, that's it." He could run his big hand down over the flank of a steer and say, almost to the pound, what he would weigh on the scales or he could look at a calf or a yearling and say, "He'll do," and he would do. A steer is a steer. He isn't supposed to do anything but make beef.

There was Don, the oldest son of the Grey family. He was so evidently destined to be a Grey, to be another like his father. He had long been a star in the 4H Club of the Virginia county and, even as a lad of nine and ten, had won prizes at steer judging. At twelve he had produced, no one helping him, doing all the work himself, more bushels of corn on an acre of land than any other boy in the State.

It was all a little amazing, even a bit queer to Mary Grey, being as she was a girl peculiarly conscious, so old and young, so aware. There was Don, the older brother, big and strong of body, like the father, and there was the young brother Ted. Ordinarily, in the ordinary course of life, she being what she was—female—it would have been quite natural and right for her to have given her young girl's admiration to Don but she didn't. For some reason, Don barely existed for her. He was outside, not in it, while for her Ted, the seemingly weak one of the family, was everything.

Still there Don was, so big of body, so quiet, so apparently sure of himself. The father had begun, as a young cattle man, with the two hundred acres, and now he had the twelve hundred. What would Don Grey do when he started? Already he knew, although he didn't say anything, that he wanted to start. He wanted to run things, be his own boss. His father had offered to send him away to college, to an agricultural college, but he wouldn't go. "No. I can learn more here," he said.

Already there was a contest, always kept under the surface, between the father and son. It concerned ways of doing things, decisions to be made. As yet the son always surrendered.

It is like that in a family, little isolated groups formed within the larger group, jealousies, concealed hatreds, silent battles secretly going on—among the Greys, Mary and Ted, Don and his father, the mother and the two younger children, Gladys, a girl child of six now, who adored her brother Don, and Harry, a boy child of two.

She had sensed something concerning her brother Ted. It was because he was as he was, having that kind of a heart, a heart likely at any moment to stop beating, leaving him dead, cut down like a young tree. The others in the Grey family, that is to say, the older ones, the mother and father and an older brother, Don, who was eighteen now, recognized something as belonging to the two children, being, as it were, between them, but the recognition wasn't very definite. People in your own family are likely at any moment to do strange, sometimes hurtful things to you. You have to watch them. Ted and Mary had both found that out.

The brother Don was like the father, already at eighteen almost a grown man. He was that sort, the kind people speak of saying: "He's a good man. He'll make a good solid dependable man." The father, when he was a

young man, never drank, never went chasing the girls,
was never wild. There had been enough wild young ones
in the Rich Valley when he was a lad. Some of them had
inherited big farms and had lost them, gambling, drinking, fooling with fast horses and chasing after the
women. It had been almost a Virginia tradition, but John
Grey was a land man. All the Greys were. There were
other large cattle farms owned by Greys up and down the
valley.

John Grey, every one said, was a natural cattle man. He
knew beef cattle, of the big so-called export type, how to
pick and feed them to make beef. He knew how and
where to get the right kind of young stock to turn into his
fields. It was blue-grass country. Big beef cattle went
directly off the pastures to market. The Grey farm contained over twelve hundred acres, most of it in blue grass.

The father was a land man, land hungry. He had
begun, as a cattle farmer, with a small place, inherited
from his father, some two hundred acres, lying next to
what was then the big Aspinwahl place and, after he
began, he never stopped getting more land. He kept
cutting in on the Aspinwahls who were a rather horsey,
fast lot. They thought of themselves as Virginia aristocrats, having, as they weren't so modest about pointing
out, a family going back and back, family tradition, guests
always being entertained, fast horses kept, money being
bet on fast horses. John Grey getting their land, now
twenty acres, then thirty, then fifty, until at last he got the
old Aspinwahl house, with one of the Aspinwahl girls,
not a young one, not one of the best-looking ones, as wife.
The Aspinwahl place was down, by that time, to less than
a hundred acres, but he went on, year after year, always
being careful and shrewd, making every penny count,
never wasting a cent, adding and adding to what was now

the Grey place. The former Aspinwahl house was a large old brick house with fireplaces in all the rooms and was very comfortable.

As for Mary and Ted, they lived within their own world, but their own world had not been established without a struggle. The point was that Ted, having the heart that might at any moment stop beating, was always being treated tenderly by the others. Only Mary understood that—how it infuriated and hurt him.

"No, Ted, I wouldn't do that.

"Now, Ted, do be careful."

Sometimes Ted went white and trembling with anger, Don, the father, the mother, all keeping at him like that. It didn't matter what he wanted to do, learn to drive one of the two family cars, climb a tree to find a bird's nest, run a race with Mary. Naturally, being on a farm, he wanted to try his hand at breaking a colt, beginning with him, getting a saddle on, having it out with him. "No, Ted. You can't." He had learned to swear, picking it up from the farm-hands and from boys at the country school. "Hell! Goddam!" he said to Mary. Only Mary understood how he felt, and she had not put the matter very definitely into words, not even to herself. It was one of the things that made her old when she was so young. It made her stand aside from the others of the family, aroused in her a curious determination. "They shall not." She caught herself saying the words to herself. "They shall not.

"If he is to have but a few years of life, they shall not spoil what he is to have. Why should they make him die, over and over, day after day?" The thoughts in her did not become so definite. She had resentment against the others. She was like a soldier, standing guard over Ted.

The two children drew more and more away, into their

own world and only once did what Mary felt come to the surface. That was with the mother.

It was on an early Summer day and Ted and Mary were playing in the rain. They were on a side porch of the house, where the water came pouring down from the eaves. At a corner of the porch there was a great stream, and first Ted and then Mary dashed through it, returning to the porch with clothes soaked and water running in streams from soaked hair. There was something joyous, the feel of the cold water on the body, under clothes, and they were shrieking with laughter when the mother came to the door. She looked at Ted. There was fear and anxiety in her voice. "Oh, Ted, you know you mustn't, you mustn't." Just that. All the rest implied. Nothing said to Mary. There it was. "Oh, Ted, you mustn't. You mustn't run hard, climb trees, ride horses. The least shock to you may do it." It was the old story again, and, of course, Ted understood. He went white and trembled. Why couldn't the rest understand that was a hundred times worse for him? On that day, without answering his mother, he ran off the porch and through the rain toward the barns. He wanted to go hide himself from every one. Mary knew how he felt.

She got suddenly very old and very angry. The mother and daughter stood looking at each other, the woman nearing fifty and the child of fourteen. It was getting everything in the family reversed. Mary felt that but felt she had to do something. "You should have more sense, Mother," she said seriously. She also had gone white. Her lips trembled. "You mustn't do it any more. Don't you ever do it again."

"What, child?" There was astonishment and half anger in the mother's voice. "Always making him think of it," Mary said. She wanted to cry but didn't.

The mother understood. There was a queer tense moment before Mary also walked off, toward the barns, in the rain. It wasn't all so clear. The mother wanted to fly at the child, perhaps shake her for daring to be so impudent. A child like that to decide things — to dare to reprove her mother. There was so much implied — even that Ted be allowed to die, quickly, suddenly, rather than that death, danger of sudden death, be brought again and again to his attention. There were values in life, implied by a child's words: "Life, what is it worth? Is death the most terrible thing?" The mother turned and went silently into the house while Mary, going to the barns, presently found Ted. He was in an empty horse stall, standing with his back to the wall, staring. There were no explanations. "Well," Ted said presently, and, "Come on, Ted," Mary replied. It was necessary to do something, even perhaps more risky than playing in the rain. The rain was already passing. "Let's take off our shoes," Mary said. Going barefoot was one of the things forbidden Ted. They took their shoes off and, leaving them in the barn, went into an orchard. There was a small creek below the orchard, a creek that went down to the river and now it would be in flood. They went into it and once Mary got swept off her feet so that Ted had to pull her out. She spoke then. "I told Mother," she said, looking serious.

"What?" Ted said. "Gee, I guess maybe I saved you from drowning," he added.

"Sure you did," said Mary. "I told her to let you alone." She grew suddenly fierce. "They've all got to — they've got to let you alone," she said.

There was a bond. Ted did his share. He was imaginative and could think of plenty of risky things to do. Perhaps the mother spoke to the father and to Don, the

older brother. There was a new inclination in the family
to keep hands off the pair, and the fact seemed to give the
two children new room in life. Something seemed to
open out. There was a little inner world created, always,
every day, being re-created, and in it there was a kind of
new security. It seemed to the two children—they could
not have put their feeling into words—that, being in their
own created world, feeling a new security there, they
could suddenly look out at the outside world and see, in a
new way, what was going on out there in the world that
belonged also to others.

It was a world to be thought about, looked at, a world of
drama too, the drama of human relations, outside their
own world, in a family, on a farm, in a farmhouse....On a
farm, calves and yearling steers arriving to be fattened,
great heavy steers going off to market, colts being broken
to work or to saddle, lambs born in the late Winter. The
human side of life was more difficult, to a child often
incomprehensible, but after the speech to the mother, on
the porch of the house that day when it rained, it seemed
to Mary almost as though she and Ted had set up a new
family. Everything about the farm, the house and the
barns got nicer. There was a new freedom. The two
children walked along a country road, returning to the
farm from school in the late afternoon. There were other
children in the road but they managed to fall behind or
they got ahead. There were plans made. "I'm going to be
a nurse when I grow up," Mary said. She may have
remembered dimly the woman nurse, from the county-
seat town, who had come to stay in the house when Ted
was so ill. Ted said that as soon as he could—it would be
when he was younger yet than Don was now — he intended to leave and go out West ... far out, he said. He
wanted to be a cowboy or a bronco-buster or something,

and, that failing, he thought he would be a railroad engineer. The railroad that went down through the Rich Valley crossed a corner of the Grey farm, and, from the road in the afternoon, they could sometimes see trains, quite far away, the smoke rolling up. There was a faint rumbling noise, and, on clear days they could see the flying piston rods of the engines.

As for the two stumps in the field near the house, they were what was left of two oak trees. The children had known the trees. They were cut one day in the early Fall.

There was a back porch to the Grey house—the house that had once been the seat of the Aspinwahl family—and from the porch steps a path led down to a stone spring house. A spring came out of the ground just there, and there was a tiny stream that went along the edge of a field, past two large barns and out across a meadow to a creek— called a "branch" in Virginia, and the two trees stood close together beyond the spring house and the fence.

They were lusty trees, their roots down in the rich, always damp soil, and one of them had a great limb that came down near the ground, so that Ted and Mary could climb into it and out another limb into its brother tree, and in the Fall, when other trees, at the front and side of the house, had shed their leaves, blood-red leaves still clung to the two oaks. They were like dry blood on gray days, but on other days, when the sun came out, the trees flamed against distant hills. The leaves clung, whispering and talking when the wind blew, so that the trees themselves seemed carrying on a conversation.

John Grey had decided he would have the trees cut. At first it was not a very definite decision. "I think I'll have them cut," he announced.

"But why?" his wife asked. The trees meant a good deal

to her. They had been planted, just in that spot, by her grandfather, she said, having in mind just a certain effect. "You see how, in the Fall, when you stand on the back porch, they are so nice against the hills." She spoke of the trees, already quite large, having been brought from a distant woods. Her mother had often spoken of it. The man, her grandfather, had a special feeling for trees. "An Aspinwahl would do that," John Grey said. "There is enough yard, here about the house, and enough trees. They do not shade the house or the yard. An Aspinwahl would go to all that trouble for trees and then plant them where grass might be growing." He had suddenly determined, a half-formed determination in him suddenly hardening. He had perhaps heard too much of the Aspinwahls and their ways. The conversation regarding the trees took place at the table, at the noon hour, and Mary and Ted heard it all.

It began at the table and was carried on afterwards out of doors, in the yard back of the house. The wife had followed her husband out. He always left the table suddenly and silently, getting quickly up and going out heavily, shutting doors with a bang as he went. "Don't, John," the wife said, standing on the porch and calling to her husband. It was a cold day but the sun was out and the trees were like great bonfires against gray distant fields and hills. The older son of the family, young Don, the one so physically like the father and apparently so like him in every way, had come out of the house with the mother, followed by the two children, Ted and Mary, and at first Don said nothing, but, when the father did not answer the mother's protest but started toward the barn, he also spoke. What he said was obviously the determining thing, hardening the father.

To the two other children — they had walked a little

aside and stood together watching and listening—there was something. There was their own child's world. "Let us alone and we'll let you alone." It wasn't as definite as that. Most of the definite thoughts about what happened in the yard that afternoon came to Mary Grey long afterwards, when she was a grown woman. At the moment there was merely a sudden sharpening of the feeling of isolation, a wall between herself and Ted and the others. The father, even then perhaps, seen in a new light, Don and the mother seen in a new light.

There was something, a driving destructive thing in life, in all relationships between people. All of this felt dimly that day—she always believed both by herself and Ted—but only thought out long afterwards, after Ted was dead. There was the farm her father had won from the Aspinwahls — greater persistence, greater shrewdness. In a family, little remarks dropped from time to time, an impression slowly built up. The father, John Grey, was a successful man. He had acquired. He owned. He was the commander, the one having power to do his will. And the power had run out and covered, not only other human lives, impulses in others, wishes, hungers in others ... he himself might not have, might not even understand ... but it went far out beyond that. It was, curiously, the power also of life and death. Did Mary Grey think such thought at that moment? ... ? She couldn't have. ... Still there was her own peculiar situation, her relationship with her brother Ted, who was to die.

Ownership that gave curious rights, dominances — fathers over children, men and women over lands, houses, factories in cities, fields. "I will have the trees in that orchard cut. They produce apples but not of the right sort. There is no money in apples of that sort any more."

"But, Sir...you see...look...the trees there against that hill, against the sky."

"Nonsense. Sentimentality."

Confusion.

It would have been such nonsense to think of the father of Mary Grey as a man without feeling. He had struggled hard all his life, perhaps, as a young man, gone without things wanted, deeply hungered for. Some one has to manage things in this life. Possessions mean power, the right to say, "do this" or "do that." If you struggle long and hard for a thing it becomes infinitely sweet to you.

Was there a kind of hatred between the father and the older son of the Grey family? "You are one also who has this thing—the impulse to power, so like my own. Now you are young and I am growing old." Admiration mixed with fear. If you would retain power it will not do to admit fear.

The young Don was so curiously like the father. There were the same lines about the jaws, the same eyes. They were both heavy men. Already the young man walked like the father, slammed doors as did the father. There was the same curious lack of delicacy of thought and touch — the heaviness that plows through, gets things done. When John Grey had married Louise Aspinwahl he was already a mature man, on his way to success. Such men do not marry young and recklessly. Now he was nearing sixty and there was the son — so like himself, having the same kind of strength.

Both land lovers, possession lovers. "It is my farm, my house, my horses, cattle, sheep." Soon now, another ten years, fifteen at the most, and the father would be ready for death. "See, already my hand slips a little. All of this to go out of my grasp." He, John Grey, had not got all of these possessions so easily. It had taken much patience, much persistence. No one but himself would ever quite know. Five, ten, fifteen years of work and saving, getting the Aspinwahl farm piece by piece. "The fools!" They had liked to think of themselves as aristocrats, throwing the land away, now twenty acres, now thirty, now fifty.

Raising horses that could never plow an acre of land.

And they had robbed the land too, had never put anything back, doing nothing to enrich it, build it up. Such a one thinking: "I'm an Aspinwahl, a gentleman. I do not soil my hands at the plow.

"Fools who do not know the meaning of land owned, possessions, money — responsibility. It is they who are second-rate men."

He had got an Aspinwahl for a wife and, as it had turned out, she was the best, the smartest and, in the end, the best-looking one of the lot.

And now there was his son, standing at the moment near the mother. They had both come down off the porch. It would be natural and right for this one — he being what he already was, what he would become — for him, in his turn, to come into possession, to take comand.

There would be, of course, the rights of the other children. If you have the stuff in you (John Grey felt that his son Don had) there is a way to manage. You buy the others out, make arrangements. There was Ted — he wouldn't be alive — and Mary and the two younger children. "The better for you if you have to struggle."

All of this, the implication of the moment of sudden struggle between a father and son, coming slowly afterwards to the man's daughter, as yet little more than a child. Does the drama take place when the seed is put into the ground or afterwards when the plant has pushed out of the ground and the bud breaks open, or still later, when the fruit ripens? There were the Greys with their ability—slow, saving, able, determined, patient. Why had they superseded the Aspinwahls in the Rich Valley? Aspinwahl blood also in the two children, Mary and Ted.

There was an Aspinwahl man—called "Uncle Fred," a brother to Louise Grey — who came sometimes to the farm. He was a rather striking-looking, tall old man with a gray Vandyke beard and a mustache, somewhat shabbily dressed but always with an indefinable air of class. He came from the county-seat town, where he lived now with a daughter who had married a merchant, a polite courtly old man who always froze into a queer silence in the presence of his sister's husband.

The son Don was standing near the mother on the day in the Fall, and the two children, Mary and Ted, stood apart.

"Don't, John," Louise Grey said again. The father, who had started away toward the barns, stopped.

"Well, I guess I will."

"No, you won't," said young Don, speaking suddenly. There was a queer fixed look in his eyes. It had flashed into life — something that was between the two men: "I possess" ... "I will possess." The father wheeled and looked sharply at the son and then ignored him.

For a moment the mother continued pleading.

"But why, why?"

"They make too much shade. The grass does not grow."

"But there is so much grass, so many acres of grass."

John Grey was answering his wife, but now again he looked at his son. There were unspoken words flying back and forth.

"I possess. I am in command here. What do you mean by telling me that I won't?"

"Ha! So! You possess now but soon I will possess."

"I'll see you in hell first."

"You fool! Not yet! Not yet!"

None of the words, set down above, was spoken at the moment, and afterwards the daughter Mary never did remember the exact words that had passed between the two men. There was a sudden quick flash of determination in Don — even perhaps sudden determination to stand by the mother — even perhaps something else — a feeling in the young Don out of the Aspinwahl blood in him—for the moment tree love superseding grass love—grass that would fatten steers. ...

Winner of 4H Club prizes, champion young corn-raiser, judge of steers, land lover, possession lover.

"You won't," Don said again.

"Won't what?"

"Won't cut those trees."

The father said nothing more at the moment but walked away from the little group toward the barns. The sun was still shining brightly. There was a sharp cold little wind. The two trees were like bonfires lighted against distant hills.

It was the noon hour and there were two men, both young, employees on the farm, who lived in a small tenant house beyond the barns. One of them, a man with a harelip, was married and the other, a rather handsome silent young man, boarded with him. They had just come from the midday meal and were going toward one of the barns. It was the beginning of the Fall corn-cutting time and they would be going together to a distant field to cut corn.

The father went to the barn and returned with the two men. They brought axes and a long cross-cut saw. "I want you to cut those two trees." There was something, a blind,

even stupid determination in the man, John Grey. And at
that moment his wife, the mother of his children...There
was no way any of the children could ever know how
many moments of the sort she had been through. She
had married John Grey. He was her man.

"If you do, Father ... " Don Grey said coldly.

"Do as I tell you! Cut those two trees!" This addressed
to the two workmen. The one who had a harelip laughed.
His laughter was like the bray of a donkey.

"Don't," said Louise Grey, but she was not addressing
her husband this time. She stepped to her son and put a
hand on his arm.

"Don't.

"Don't cross him. Don't cross my man ." Could a child
like Mary Grey comprehend? It takes time to understand
things that happen in life. Life unfolds slowly to the
mind. Mary was standing with Ted, whose young face was
white and tense. Death at his elbow. At any moment. At
any moment.

"I have been through this a hundred times. That is the
way this man I married has succeeded. Nothing stops
him. I married him; I have had my children by him.

"We women choose to submit.

"This is my affair, more than yours, Don, my son."

A woman hanging onto her thing—the family, created
about her.

The son not seeing things with her eyes. He shook off
his mother's hand, lying on his arm. Louise Grey was
younger than her husband, but, if he was now nearing
sixty, she was drawing near fifty. At the moment she
looked very delicate and fragile. There was something, at
the moment, in her bearing....Was there, after all, something in blood, the Aspinwahl blood?

In a dim way perhaps, at the moment, the child Mary

did comprehend. Women and their men. For her then, at
that time, there was but one male, the child Ted. Afterwards she remembered how he looked at that moment,
the curiously serious old look on his young face. There
was even, she thought later, a kind of contempt for both
the father and brother, as though he might have been
saying to himself—he couldn't really have been saying it
—he was too young: "Well, we'll see. This is something.
These foolish ones—my father and my brother. I myself
haven't long to live. I'll see what I can, while I do live."

The brother Don stepped over near to where his father
stood.

"If you do, Father ... " he said again.

"Well?"

"I'll walk off this farm and I'll never come back."

"All right. Go then."

The father began directing the two men who had
begun cutting the trees, each man taking a tree. The
young man with the harelip kept laughing, the laughter
like the bray of a donkey. "Stop that," the father said
sharply, and the sound ceased abruptly. The son Don
walked away, going rather aimlessly toward the barn. He
approached one of the barns and then stopped. The
mother, white now, half ran into the house.

The son returned toward the house, passing the two
younger children without looking at them, but did not
enter. The father did not look at him. He went hesitatingly along a path at the front of the house and through a
gate and into a road. The road ran for several miles down
through the valley and then, turning, went over a mountain to the county-seat town.

As it happened, only Mary saw the son Don when he
returned to the farm. There were three or four tense

days. Perhaps, all the time, the mother and son had been secretly in touch. There was a telephone in the house. The father stayed all day in the fields, and when he was in the house was silent.

Mary was in one of the barns on the day when Don came back and when the Father and son met. It was an odd meeting.

The son came, Mary always afterwards thought, rather sheepishly. The father came out of a horse's stall. He had been throwing corn to work horses. Neither the father nor son saw Mary. There was a car parked in the barn and she had crawled into the driver's seat, her hands on the steering wheel, pretending she was driving.

"Well," the father said. If he felt triumphant, he did not show his feeling.

"Well," said the son, "I have come back."

"Yes, I see," the father said. "They are cutting corn." He walked toward the barn door and then stopped. "It will be yours soon now," he said. "You can be boss then."

He said no more and both men went away, the father toward the distant fields and the son toward the house. Mary was afterwards quite sure that nothing more was ever said.

What had the father meant?

"When it is yours you can be boss." It was too much for the child. Knowledge comes slowly. It meant:

"You will be in command, and for you, in your turn, it will be necessary to assert.

"Such men as we are cannot fool with delicate stuff. Some men are meant to command and others must obey. You can make them obey in your turn.

"There is a kind of death.

"Something in you must die before you can possess and command."

There was, so obviously, more than one kind of death. For Don Grey one kind and for the younger brother Ted, soon now perhaps, another.

Mary ran out of the barn that day, wanting eagerly to get out into the light, and afterwards, for a long time, she did not try to think her way through what had happened. She and her brother Ted did, however, afterwards, before he died, discuss quite often the two trees. They went on a cold day and put their fingers on the stumps, but the stumps were cold. Ted kept asserting that only men got their legs and arms cut off, and she protested. They continued doing things that had been forbidden Ted to do, but no one protested, and, a year or two later, when he died, he died during the night in his bed.

But while he lived, there was always, Mary afterwards thought, a curious sense of freedom, something that belonged to him that made it good, a great happiness, to be with him. It was, she finally thought, because having to die his kind of death, he never had to make the surrender his brother had made—to be sure of possessions, success, his time to command—would never have to face the more subtle and terrible death that had come to his older brother.

The Corn Planting

The farmers who come to our town to trade are a part of the town life. Saturday is the big day. Often the children come to the high school in town.

It is so with Hatch Hutchenson. Although his farm, some three miles from town, is small, it is known to be one of the best-kept and best-worked places in all our section. Hatch is a little gnarled old figure of a man. His place is on the Scratch Gravel Road and there are plenty of poorly kept places out that way.

Hatch's place stands out. The little frame house is always kept painted, the trees in his orchard are whitened with lime halfway up the trunks, and the barn and sheds are in repair, and his fields are always clean-looking.

Hatch is nearly seventy. He got a rather late start in life. His father, who owned the same farm, was a Civil War man and came home badly wounded, so that, although he lived a long time after the war, he couldn't work much. Hatch was the only son and stayed at home, working the place until his father died. Then, when he was nearing fifty, he married a schoolteacher of forty, and they had a son. The schoolteacher was a small one like Hatch. After they married, they both stuck close to the land. They seemed to fit into their farm life as certain people fit into the clothes they wear. I have noticed something about people who make a go of marriage. They grow more and more alike. They even grow to look alike.

Their one son, Will Hutchenson, was a small but remarkably strong boy. He came to our high school in town and pitched on our town baseball team. He was a fellow always cheerful, bright and alert, and a great favorite with all of us.

For one thing, he began as a young boy to make amusing little drawings. It was a talent. He made drawings of fish and pigs and cows, and they looked like people you knew. I never did know, before, that people could look so much like cows and horses and pigs and fish.

When he had finished in the town high school, Will went to Chicago, where his mother had a cousin living, and he became a student in the Art Institute out there. Another young fellow from our town was also in Chicago. He really went two years before Will did. His name is Hal Weyman, and he was a student at the University of Chicago. After he graduated, he came home and got a job as principal of our high school.

Hal and Will Hutchenson hadn't been close friends before, Hal being several years older than Will, but in Chicago they got together, went together to see plays, and, as Hal later told me, they had a good many long talks.

I got it from Hal that, in Chicago, as at home here when he was a young boy, Will was immediately popular. He was good-looking, so the girls in the art school liked him, and he had a straightforwardness that made him popular with all the young fellows.

Hal told me that Will was out to some party nearly every night, and right away he began to sell some of his amusing little drawings and to make money. The drawings were used in advertisements, and he was well paid.

He even began to send some money home. You see, after Hal came back here, he used to go quite often out to the Hutchenson place to see Will's father and mother. He would walk or drive out there in the afternoon or on summer evenings and sit with them. The talk was always of Will.

Hal said it was touching how much the father and mother depended on their one son, how much they talked about him and dreamed of his future. They had never been people who went about much with the town folks or even with their neighbors. They were of the sort who work all the time, from early morning till late in the evenings, and on moonlight nights, Hal said, and after the little old wife had got the supper, they often went out into the fields and worked again.

You see, by this time old Hatch was nearing seventy and his wife would have been ten years younger. Hal said that whenever he went out to the farm they quit work and came to sit with him. They might be in one of the fields, working together, but when they saw him in the road, they came running.They had got a letter from Will. He wrote every week.

The little old mother would come running following the father. "We got another letter, Mr. Weyman," Hatch would cry, and then his wife, quite breathless, would say the same thing, "Mr. Weyman, we got a letter."

The letter would be brought out at once and read aloud. Hal said the letters were always delicious. Will larded them with little sketches. There were humorous drawings of people he had seen or been with, rivers of automobiles on Michigan Avenue in Chicago, a policeman at a street crossing, young stenographers hurrying into office buildings. Neither of the old people had ever been to the city and they were curious and eager. They wanted the drawings explained, and Hal said they were like two children wanting to know every little detail Hal could remember about their son's life in the big city. He was always at them to come there on a visit and they would spend hours talking of that.

"Of course," Hatch said, "we couldn't go."

"How could we?" he said. He had been on that one little farm since he was a boy When he was a young fellow, his father was an invalid and so Hatch had to run things. A farm, if you run it right, is very exacting. You have to fight weeds all the time. There are the farm animals to take care of. "Who would milk our cows?" Hatch said. The idea of anyone but him or his wife touching one of the Hutchenson cows seemed to hurt him. While he was alive, he didn't want anyone else plowing one of his fields, tending his corn, looking after things about the barn. He felt that way about his farm. It was a thing you couldn't explain, Hal said. He seemed to understand the two old people.

It was a spring night, past midnight, when Hal came to my house and told me the news. In our town we have a night telegraph operator at the railroad station and Hal got a wire. It was really addressed to Hatch Hutchenson, but the operator brought it to Hal. Will Hutchenson was dead, had been killed. It turned out later that he was at a party with some other young fellows and there might have been some drinking. Anyway, the car was wrecked, and Will Hutchenson was killed. The operator wanted Hal to go out and take the message to Hatch and his wife, and Hal wanted me to go along.

I offered to take my car, but Hal said no. "Let's walk out," he said. He wanted to put off the moment, I could

see that. So we did walk. It was early spring, and I remember every moment of the silent walk we took, the
little leaves just coming on the trees, the little streams we
crossed, how the moonlight made the water seem alive.
We loitered and loitered, not talking, hating to go on.

Then we got out there, and Hal went to the front door
of the farmhouse while I stayed in the road. I heard a dog
bark, away off somewhere. I heard a child crying in some
distant house. I think that Hal, after he got to the front
door of the house, must have stood there for ten minutes,
hating to knock.

Then he did knock, and the sound his fist made on the
door seemed terrible. It seemed like guns going off. Old
Hatch came to the door, and I heard Hal tell him. I know
what happened. Hal had been trying, all the way out
from town, to think up words to tell the old couple in
some gentle way, but when it came to the scratch, he
couldn't. He blurted everything right out, right into old
Hatch's face.

That was all. Old Hatch didn't way a word. The door
was opened, he stood there in the moonlight, wearing a
funny long white nightgown, Hal told him, and the door
went shut again with a bang, and Hal was left standing
there.

He stood for a time, and then came back out into the
road to me. "Well," he said, and "Well," I said. We stood in
the road looking and listening. There wasn't a sound
from the house.

And then—it might have been ten minutes or it might
have been a half-hour—we stood silently, listening and
watching, not knowing what to do—we couldn't go away
—"I guess they are trying to get so they can believe it,"
Hal whispered to me. I got his notion all right. The two
old people must have thought of their son Will always

only in terms of life, never of death.

We stood watching and listening, and then, suddenly, after a long time, Hal touched me on the arm. "Look," he whispered. There were two white-clad figures going from the house to the barn. It turned out, you see, that old Hatch had been plowing that day. He had finished plowing and harrowing a field near the barn.

The two figures went into the barn and presently came out. They went into the field, and Hal and I crept across the farmyard to the barn and got to where we could see what was going on without being seen.

It was an incredible thing. The old man had got a hand cornplanter out of the barn and his wife had got a bag of seed corn, and there, in the moonlight, that night, after they got that news, they were planting corn.

It was a thing to curl your hair—it was so ghostly. They were both in their nightgowns. They would do a row across the field, coming quite close to us as we stood in the shadow of the barn, and then, at the end of each row, they would kneel side by side by the fence and stay silent for a time. The whole thing went on in silence. It was the first time in my life I ever understood something, and I am far from sure now that I can put down what I understood and felt that night—I mean something about the connection between certain people and the earth—a kind of silent cry, down into the earth, of these two old people, putting corn down into the earth. It was as though they were putting death down into the ground that life might grow again—something like that.

They must have been asking something of the earth, too. But what's the use? What they were up to in connection with the life in their field and the lost life in their son is something you can't very well make clear in words. All I know is that Hal and I stood the sight as long as we could, and then we crept away and went back to town, but Hatch Hutchenson and his wife must have got what they were after that night, because Hal told me that when he went out in the morning to see them and to make the arrangements for bringing their dead son home, they were both curiously quiet and Hal thought in command of themselves. Hal said he thought they had got something. "They have their farm and they have still got Will's letters to read," Hal said.